Madeline Leslie

Never give up

the news-boys

Madeline Leslie

Never give up
the news-boys

ISBN/EAN: 9783337414429

Printed in Europe, USA, Canada, Australia, Japan

Cover: Foto ©Andreas Hilbeck / pixelio.de

More available books at **www.hansebooks.com**

NEVER GIVE UP ;

OR,

THE NEWS-BOYS.

BY

MRS. MADELINE LESLIE,

AUTHOR OF "TIM THE SCISSORS-GRINDER," "EARNING AND SPENDING," "UP THE LADDER," "THE FRANKIE SERIES," "THE ROBIN SERIES," ETC.

" Cast thy bread upon the waters; for thou shalt find it after many days."

BOSTON:

GRAVES AND YOUNG;

24 CORNHILL.

NEW YORK: SHELDON AND COMPANY.

CINCINNATI: GEO. S. BLANCHARD.

1864.

To

WILLIAM A. BOOTH, ESQ.,

And other Officers of the Children's Aid Society,

EMBRACING THE NEWS-BOYS' LODGING-HOUSE
IN NEW YORK CITY,

THIS LITTLE VOLUME IS RESPECTFULLY INSCRIBED,

BY THE AUTHOR,

IN TESTIMONY OF HER HIGH APPRECIATION OF THEIR HUMANE
AND BENEVOLENT ENTERPRISES.

INTRODUCTION.

THE subject of this little volume was suggested by a visit to the humane institutions under the direction of the Children's Aid Society in the city of New York: and the author would here most gratefully acknowledge her indebtedness to the Superintendents of those institutions for copies of their annual reports, and for many of the facts contained in this narrative.

If the book encourages the inmates of those asylums to adopt the motto on its title-page, and "NEVER GIVE UP" the hope nor the effort of attaining to stations of usefulness and honor; and if it serve in any humble degree

to commend these humane and benevolent enterprises to the increased confidence and patronage
of the Christian public, its object will be attained.

WELLESLEY, SEPTEMBER, 1862.

CONTENTS.

CHAPTER IX.

CHAPTER X.

CHAPTER XI.

CHAPTER XII.

CHAPTER XIII.

CHAPTER XIV.

CHAPTER XV.

CHAPTER XVI.

CHAPTER XVII.

CHAPTER XVIII.

CHAPTER XIX.

NEVER GIVE UP.

CHAPTER I.

JACK THE NEWS-BOY.

ORNING ede-shun, Journal o' Commerce
—last speech and execu-tion o' Professor
Watson."

I was walking leisurely through Broadway
when these words, drawled out by a score of
news-boys, arrested my attention. The public
was at this time greatly excited by this tragedy;
and I, in common with others, was eager to
learn anything new that had transpired concerning it. I turned, therefore, to one of the
little fellows who was pulling my coat, pur-
chased a paper, and should probably have
never thought of him again, had it not been

11

for the following slight circumstance, which, I love to reflect had an important bearing on the future history of the boy.

In paying him the four cents which were his due, I counted into his hand some loose coppers I found in my pocket; and among them, it seemed, one sixpence and a shilling-piece. I turned away, and was several steps from him, when he ran after me and, touching my elbow, said, " Sir, you gave me too much."

" Ah, did I ? let me see ; are you sure I gave you all that ? "

" Yes, sir, I'm sure."

The words that rose to my lips were, " Keep them, my lad; I'm glad you're so honest." But there was something in his eager, wistful look that arrested my attention, and I said, " Well, you see that office over there."

" The one with the sign ' E. O. Sennott ? ' "

" Yes, that's my name; come up there after you sell your papers : I want to talk with you."

" Wont you take the money, sir ? "

" You can bring it with you." " This will put his honesty to a further test," I said to myself, as I hurried on.

I was soon absorbed in my paper, and I had quite forgotten my morning acquaintance, when I heard a quick step on the stairs, followed by a low knock at my office door, and presently the little news-boy stood before me.

" Take a seat," I said, but could not help smiling when I saw him perched on a high stool on which my clerk sat at the desk, his bare feet dangling under him.

" Are you one of Mr. Rogers's boys ? " I asked.

" No, sir. I'm Jack Stetson; I used to sell candy ; but now I'm promoted to the Journal o' Commerce."

" I mean," I added, with a smile, " are you one of the Lodging-House boys, — the one Mr. Rogers's keeps ? "

"Oh no, sir!" returning the smile; "the old woman isn't dead yet."

"What old woman?"

"My mother, sir."

"And is she sick?"

His voice changed at once, and there was the same earnest gaze which fixed my attention in the morning.

"Yes, sir; she says she's most got through."

"And who supports her?"

"I do, sir; I take care of her every night."

"How old are you, Jack?"

"Eleven, come Christmas."

My thoughts reverted, on the instant, to my own boy, within a few months of the same age, but whom his mother thought too young to walk in the street by himself. Yet here was a lad left to make his own way in the world; aye, and to support his mother, too.

"Here's the money, sir," he said, opening

his hand, which had been tightly closed over the silver pieces.

I took them from him and laid them on the table. There was not the slightest shade of disappointment visible on his good-humored face.

" I am glad to see you are honest, Jack. It proves to me that you have a good mother, who has carefully taught you what is right."

He laughed. " The boys called me spooney for not keeping the money."

" Well, you see they were mistaken, for you have made a good friend by your honesty. But about your mother — don't you think a doctor could do her good?"

" She says not, sir. She says she's most through."

" And does she remain alone, while you are selling your papers?"

" Yes, sir, mostly; but there's a woman on our flight who is kind to her, she and her daughters."

" Where do you live ? "

He gave me the street and number, which I
made a memorandum of on the back of a card.

A neighboring clock sounded ten, when, with
a start, Jack said, " It's my school-time, sir ;
shall I go ? "

" Yes ; but I am surprised that you can
attend school."

" The old woman keeps me at it," he said,
laughing and nodding his good-bye.

After dinner I sat in a luxurious easy chair,
my feet lazily stretched upon another, just
falling into forgetfulness of the world and its
cares, when, with a start, I remembered a re-
solve I had made to visit the news-boy. It
was really an effort to give up the fifteen minutes usually devoted to Somnus ; but I con-
quered myself, and, calling my only son Alfred,
we sallied forth in quest of the widow Stetson.

It was not a difficult search. On entering
the street I looked for the number Jack had

designated, and I inquired for a sick woman
by the name of Stetson, and was directed to the
fourth flight, right-hand door.

I knocked, and heard a feeble voice answer,
" Come in."

The woman was sitting up in bed mending
a boy's jacket; but it was easy to see the task
was beyond her strength.

" I am a friend to Jack," I said at once,
" and promised him I would call and see
you."

" If you and the young gentleman will
please take seats, sir," she went on, in a hesitating voice, "I am too sick to rise."

" Jack is at school, I suppose."

" Yes, sir. He is obliged to be somewhat
irregular ; but I want him to get all the learning he can."

There was the same look in the eye which
she bent on me as had interested me in her
son. I answered, " Jack is a good boy," and
2

repeated the incident of the morning. My attention was so engaged in noticing how eagerly Alfred swallowed the story, that not until I heard a quick sob did I perceive how much the mother was affected.

She wiped her eyes with the corner of the sheet slyly, as if ashamed of her emotion, when I added, " I'm sure he will reward you for the pains you have taken to teach him his duty."

" Thank you, sir. Nothing you could have told me would have given so much pleasure." Her voice shook, but became firmer as she added, " Jack is a good boy, and its my prayer day and night that, when I'm gone, he may remember my instructions. I'm most through, sir, and I'm glad to go; but it's hard leaving a child like him. "

" But you remember God's promises to the fatherless, especially to the children of those who put their trust in him : ' I will be a God to thee, and to thy seed after thee.' The children of thy servants shall continue, and their seed shall be established before thee.'"

"Yes, sir," she answered, her eyes kindling, and another, 'I will pour my blessing upon thine offspring.' These are precious indeed, and many a night have I feasted my soul upon them. But, sir, my faith is often weak. I am a poor, feeble creature at best, and sometimes I lose hold of God's promises, and then I tremble at the thought of leaving my boy alone to fight his battle with the world."

Alfred drew closer to my side, and clasped my hand. "Would my faith conquer in such an hour?" was a question which forced itself upon me.

There was something in the appearance and language of the woman which denoted that at some time in her life she had been in happier circumstances. I hinted the fact, and she responded frankly.

"I was adopted by a lady in this city when my parents died, and was kept at school till my eighteenth year. She meant to prepare me to be a teacher, but soon after that time she was taken sick, and I would not leave her; I nursed her two years, when she died, leaving me three hundred dollars. Soon after I was married, and lived most happily until Jack reached his fifth summer, when my husband, who was a carpenter, fell from the scaffolding and received such an injury on his head that he lived but a few days.

" His death was a dreadful shock to me; but I bore up as well as I could, for the sake of our little boy. At that time I had not learned the comfort of going to my Saviour with all my trials; but Mr. Stetson's consistent example and his earnest prayers for me had not been in vain. He had not been gone but a few months before I was enabled to cast myself, my poor, bleeding heart and all its burdens, at the foot of the cross."

"For a number of years I earned a comfortable support by selling candy, which I made for the little boys to sell again in the streets, keeping Jack at school; but before he was ten he insisted he was old enough to earn money for me, and did so with the others, until I was so sick I was obliged to give up. Then he obtained papers to sell, while I sewed for the slopshops; and I have great reason to be thankful that he has not been obliged to give up his learning."

"He is in school now, I suppose," I remarked, as she ceased speaking.

A pleasant smile lighted her face.

"Yes, sir; he brought me an orange, and placed my drink where I could reach it, and then ran off again. O; sir, it's a great trial to leave such a boy exposed to the temptations of a city like this."

I did not answer, for at this moment the door opened softly and a youthful face peeped in, but was immediately withdrawn.

" She is the daughter of the woman who lives in the opposite chamber," said Mrs. Stetson, in answer to my look of inquiry.

" She or her mother comes in, many times in the day to see whether I want anything. In return Jack brings from the shop and carries back their bundles of work."

" I shall ask our family physician to call and see you," I said, rising, and if you need anything more than the few things I shall send here, Jack knows my office, and can come to me there."

All this time I noticed that Alfred stood gazing alternately at me and the widow, his large eyes wearing that spiritual look which so often reminded me of his dear sister who was now resting in the bosom of her Saviour. As I rose, he whispered, " Wont you pray, father ?"

I repeated his request, which the woman earnestly seconded, when, approaching nearer to the bed, we poured our united supplications into the ear of the Most High.

CHAPTER II.

JACK LEFT AN ORPHAN.

IT was several weeks after the occurrence
of the above incidents, when, one morning,
as I happened to be looking from my office-
window, I saw a number of boys on the opposite pavement gathered about two of their
number, who were fighting " with a will." As
I stood watching them and wondering the police did not interfere, I recognized in one of
the young combatants Jack Stetson, the news-
boy.

Acting on the impulse of the moment, I took
my hat and went down stairs ; but the dispute
seemed to be rather suddenly settled ; for, when
I reached the spot, Jack was taking his papers

24

from a lad who stood by, and immediately commenced his monotonous drawl —

" Morning ede-shun Journal o' Commerce," etc.

He colored to the roots of his hair when he saw me, but held out a paper saying, " Morning edition, sir ? "

" How is your mother, Jack ? " I asked, gravely.

" She says she's most through, sir. She's been wanting to see you to thank you for — "

" Never mind that Jack. What was the matter with you this morning ? "

His eyes met mine frankly, as he said, " He charged me with stealing his papers, sir."

" But that was not true ? "

" No, indeed, sir ; I bought my papers and paid for them. He says he paid for his, and left them a moment, when they were gone."

" Did you ever steal ? "

I was sorry the moment I had asked the

question, for it occasioned such distress, I expected to hear a vehement denial; but instead
of that he answered, softly:

" Yes, sir, once."

" I'm sorry for that, Jack, and I'm sure you
must be sorry too."

" Yes, sir."

" Do you ever swear?

" Sometimes I do, sir ; but most times I
don't."

" And tell lies ? "

He drew himself up almost haughtily.

" No, sir; nobody can say as I tell lies."

" Well, Jack, it's almost time for you to go
to school, and you have still a pile of papers."

" So I have, sir;" and with a little nod he
turned away; and I presently heard his voice
some distance up the street calling out, " Morning ede-shun," etc.

When I went home I related to Alfred my
meeting with the young news-boy for whom

he felt a particular interest. He seemed quite excited with Jack's confession that he had once been guilty of stealing; but said, after thinking some time, " I'm glad he told the truth about it, father."

The next day I left the city for a fortnight. A few mornings after my return, I felt some one gently pulling my coat, and turning around saw Jack. His eyes were red with crying, though his face was very pale.

" Mother's most through," he said in a husky tone. " She's dying now, sir."

I saw that his arm was full of papers, and comprehended at once that his heart was too heavy to sell them.

" Do you know Jack ? " I asked another lad who stood close by.

" Yes, sir."

" You may sell his Journals this morning; and I will pay you for it. Do you agree to this ? "

" Yes, sir."

" Come, Jack," I said, " I will go with you
to see your mother. She may not be as bad
as you think."

His lips quivered, but he did not reply.

We were but just in time. When we entered the room, the dying woman was propped
up in bed, a chair being placed behind to keep
her in an upright position. She looked eagerly toward the door, and made a motion of
gratitude when she saw Jack.

He bounded toward the bed, and laid his
head down beside her pale hand, which he
kept kissing.

I looked in vain for any trace of the distress she had shown at our last interview. Her
countenance was fairly illumined, showing that
her soul was at peace.

The young girl I had seen before and her
mother were present, and made way for me to
come to the bed. Mrs. Stetson was almost past

speaking, but with a glance toward her son she faltered out the words, " God is good — I can trust my boy — with him — He gives me dying grace."

I repeated the promises so precious to the believer, " Thou wilt keep him in perfect peace whose mind is stayed on thee." " Though I walk through the valley of the shadow of death, I will fear no evil; for thou art with me, thy rod and thy staff they comfort me."

. She made a motion of assent, and then intimated a wish that I should pray.

We knelt around the lowly bed, and committed the dying soul to God. When we arose, death had been exchanged for victory. Only the soul's empty casement lay before us.

I was greatly affected at poor Jack's grief when he found his mother really had left him. He did not cry aloud ; but he laid his head on the table, and sobbed as if his heart was broken.

I made a few arrangements for the simple

funeral, and then left the woman to prepare
the body for the grave. Two days later, taking Alfred with me, we ascended the creaking
stairs to the chamber of the dead. The minister was already there, and the service just
about to begin.

Poor Jack sat apart from the rest, his face
very pale but calm. When the service was
completed, the coffin was removed with difficulty down the steep, narrow flights, placed in
the hearse, and then Jack took his position
behind as chief and only mourner.

All this time Alfred had watched the proceedings with absorbing interest. When he
saw the little fellow apparently deserted, he
gave one quick, earnest glance into my face,
and then, without a word, darted forward, and
pressed his small gloved hand into that of the
sorrowing news-boy.

I saw Jack's face flush at this unexpected
companionship, though neither of them spoke;

while my own heart swelled with pleasure at the thought of my boy's unaffected sympathy with grief.

In accordance with my request, the poor little orphan called in a short time at my office, when I gave him the following note to Mr. Rogers, the well-known Superintendent of the News-Boy's Lodging-House.

" DEAR SIR : — The bearer of this is a news-boy, lately deprived of his mother and his home. He has been carefully taught his duties to his Maker, and it seems especially desirable that he should enjoy the benefit of your worthy institution.

With respect, E. O. SENNOTT."

I now regularly bought my morning paper of Jack, who seemed to regard me with the most friendly feelings. Every day I was beset by Alfred for further intelligence of the news-boy, and occasionally they met at my office.

The stories Jack told of Mr. Rogers's boys, as those belonging to the Lodging-House were called, much amused us. He said they had regular games there during the evening, and a school which all were urged to attend. Each boy had a bed to himself and a comfortable supper, for which only a nominal price was paid. They were encouraged to lay aside their earnings by putting them into a bank, connected with the establishment; every cent being credited to them, for the supply of their future necessities; and every attention was paid to their moral training, which the ingenuity of the excellent Superintendent could devise.

Some of these news-boys had been outcasts from society. Taught to lie, steal, and swear from their earliest remembrance — educated in the low cunning of the most depraved part of our population — considering the one who cheated the most customers, and passed off the most old papers, as the best fellow, it was no easy task to effect, what was desired, a radical change in all these habits, and to make of these poor children of the street good and useful members of society.

The benevolent persons who organized the institution of the lodging-houses, realized that in order to stop the progress of vice, the youth of the city must be reformed and trained to habits of honesty and virtue. Mr. Rogers, who first entered on the task, was well fitted for the labor. He was firm in rebuking vice, of whatever nature, and would not allow the least infringement of the rules of the establishment. But fortunately for those who were under his care, he understood the nature of boys; and as, at proper times, he did not object to considerable noise, in spouting as they called it, or in arguing, while he endeavored to unite recreation with profit, they soon began to realize the vast improvement upon their former mode

3

of living, and to appreciate the advantage of a good home.

But I cannot give the reader a better idea of the lodging-houses, their aim, objects, and means of improvement to the friendless lads, than by quoting from the account of the good Superintendent, which I will do in the next chapter.

CHAPTER III.

"THIS Institution," says the Principal, "was founded to provide a home for all kinds of street-boys, many of whom come to us utterly penniless and destitute. Itinerant lads, such as match sellers, apple venders, button peddlers, boot-blacks, baggage carriers, paper folders, market boys, and especially news-boys; in fact, all honestly engaged in petty pursuits, or out of work, here find a home.

"We hold out the inducement of a comfortable single bed, in a well ventilated apartment, the charge for those who have means being four cents; a warm supper, free if he is in

35

early, a library, a melodeon, a savings bank,
a school-room (which serves also for chapel
and play-room), bath and wash-room, and a
private lock closet for clothes.

" By these means the majority of our inmates have been reclaimed from a vagrant life,
sleeping in market houses, hay barges, old
alleys, open stairways, ash and coal boxes,
wagons, and empty rail-way cars, or obliged to
walk the street all night, exposed to the temptations of homelessness and privation, or, of
those seminaries of evil, the drinking saloons.

" The evenings of the week are variously
passed by the boys. On Wednesday evening
there is an interesting lecture, on Thursday a
prayer-meeting, on Friday a singing-teacher
attends, and on the Sabbath there are exercises
appropriate to the day. The afternoon and
evening school occupies the rest of the week —
a brief devotional exercise closing every day.

" A free Sunday dinner is still provided by

a few benevolent individuals for all who re-
frain from work on that day. This has been
found a great inducement for withdrawing a
large number of boys from the streets, and
obviating the necessity of their working on
the Sabbath.

" Habits of economy and order are developed
by the desire to deposit as much as their
companions in the savings bank. During one
year, three hundred and thirty boys saved one
thousand two hundred and fifty-seven dollars.

" The bank is open the first day of every
month, and the depositor receives five per
cent. on his savings. We assert no control over
the money of the boys, and merely give them
counsel about the judicious disposal of it; but
they generally re-deposit it in one of the city
savings banks."

It was a habit of Mr. Rogers, when the boys
had been unusually obedient and attentive to
his wishes, to read them an interesting story.

The life of Benjamin Franklin, of Roger Sher-
man, of Benjamin West, and of many others
who, by their own persevering exertions, had
risen from being as poor as themselves, to be
eminent and useful men, stirred many a youth
to similar endeavors.

Here it was that Jack Stetson first came to
reflect that God had given him powers which
would enable him to rise from a news-boy, perhaps, to be the owner and editor of a paper.
From that hour, Jack determined to be somebody.

Weeks and months flew by, until Mrs. Stetson had been dead one year. Mrs. Holland
the widow, who with her daughters still lived in
the opposite chamber, earned a scanty support
by sewing for the slop-shops, Jack still rendering himself useful by carrying their bundles
to and fro from their employers. Edith Holland had grown to be a beautiful young lady,
for lady she was in refinement of feeling, and

even in education, though obliged by stern necessity to spend her days in bending over her almost hopeless tasks. Of late Jack, who was her stout defender, had noticed that she was growing pale and wan, and a vision of her lying weak and languid in bed, and at last breathing out her life a victim to endless stitching, as his mother had done, began to float through his mind.

Jack had a favorite among his companions at the Lodging-House, a lad two years older than himself, named Norris, to whom he confided his fears in regard to Edith. This youth was one to whom Mr. Rogers could point with a certain kind of self-gratulation, as a case of what good, moral influences, connected with kind but firm treatment, can do for boys who are apparently destined for nothing but the prison and the gallows.

When Edward Norris was first persuaded to join the youth who assembled night after

night at the Lodging-House, the restraint from
the wild freedom of the street was so irksome,
he several times broke loose and returned to
his old haunts. Again and again had Mr.
Rogers rescued him from the hands of the
police, who were carrying him to the station-
house for being engaged in a street brawl.
But circumstances had sharpened the good
man's observation, and made him a keen ob-
server of human nature. He perceived some
traits in Edward Norris which, if cultivated
and brought into action, would make a noble
man. He was not easily discouraged, therefore, when some months passed before there
was any perceptible change in the lad. His
first business was to gain Edward's confidence,
and convince him he was a true friend.

Circumstances after a time favored this
effort; for the youth was taken sick of a vio-
lent fever, and the Superintendent nursed
him with the tenderness of a parent. Though

pressed with the responsible duties of his office, he passed every moment he could command, by the humble couch of the poor boy.

As Edward became convalescent, he had time to reflect upon his situation, and to compare it with what it would have been had not the kindness of Mr. Rogers interfered in his behalf. With no home he could call his own, and not one friend in this vast city who would have interposed to benefit him, his bed would doubtless have been, as it had often been before, under the shelter of a cart on the cold pavement, where, when discovered by the police he would have been thrust into the station-house, and no doubt have died for want of care.

"Now," he thought, casting his eyes around the comfortable apartment, with the neat rows of single beds on either side of him, " here I am treated as if I were a child ; and why ? Yes, why does Mr. Rogers care for me, or for these other rude boys? It cannot be simply because he is paid for it; for he enters into our interests with all his heart and soul. It must be on account of the goodness there is in him, which makes him wish us all to be good. Well, I for one will try to please him. It's the least I can do, after all his kindness to me."

Edward Norris kept his resolution. He did try to please the Superintendent, and soon gained such an influence over his associates that he was a great aid to his benefactor. He now was as eager to enter the school-room as before he had been to avoid it. Every moment that could be gained from his business as a news-boy he spent in acquiring the rudiments of knowledge. It was astonishing how soon he learned to read and write, and what an enthusiasm he was the means of diffusing among his companions. Besides this, Mr. Rogers said he was the best agent he had for bringing news-boys to the institution. Many and many a rude

lad, the very offscouring of society, the very
ones of whom house-breakers and murderers
are made, came stealthily into the office in his
train, casting shy glances around, and ready
to escape on the first symptoms of restraint.
To such he represented in glowing colors the
state he himself was in when he first came to
the Lodging-House, and then, straightening
himself up in the dignity of a self-acquired
manhood, asked them to judge whether his situation was not every way more enviable now.

At the time our young friend, Jack Stetson,
first entered the Lodging-House, Edward was
about forming a club, as he aspiringly called
it, to argue questions put to them by their
teacher, or to declaim pieces for the interest
of the whole.

A friendship was instantly formed between
the two boys, greatly to the advantage of both.
In many things there was a great congeniality
between them. Edward was, as I have said,

older, he being fourteen, while Jack had only
reached his twelfth birth-day; but then, Jack
had received daily instruction from the lips of
a pious mother, while Edward had been sink-
ing deeper and deeper in crime, becoming
every day more of an adept in petty thefts and
deceptions, from his contact with those only
who were qualified to teach him the ways of
sin, until found and rescued by Mr. Rogers.

Jack, too, had the advantage of having
always attended to his studies, he being now a
member of one of the public schools, in the
ward to which he belonged, and, consequently,
far in advance of his older companion.

It may be supposed, therefore, that he became at once a distinguished member of the
club, and that Edward, who, as the projector
of the society, was chosen its president, should
call him out on every possible occasion.

One evening after their work for the day was
done, Jack and Ned were enjoying themselves

in the play-room, when company to visit the institution was announced; and the Superintendent cheerfully called the boys to take their places on the forms.

It was an event of very frequent occurrence for ladies and gentlemen to visit them, — the latter often making speeches to the boys, impressing some moral or religious lesson.

On this occasion, however, after some merry conversation in a low voice between them and Mr. Rogers, the Superintendent said:

" Boys, we should like this evening to be amused, and as John Smith seems to possess a talent for tragedy, we should like to see him perform."

John Smith was a lad of a peculiarly rag-tag-and-bob-tail appearance. He was at this time scratching his head and yawning in a corner; but being called by name looked up much astonished. Seeing all the boys gazing at him, he was wide awake in a moment. Taking the

floor he ran his fingers through his hair, and
with a wild stare into a vacant space, he began
in a theatrical manner:

"Come on, Romeo and Juliet!" "Give
me another horse; bind up my wounds,"
"Soft, I did but dream." "What noise is
this?" "Not dead? not yet quite dead?"
"Will thou provoke me? then have at thee,
boy!" "Back, back, and quit my sight; thy
bones are marrowless." "Oh! I die Horatio."

At the end of this conglomeration of different plays, which John had incorrectly gathered
from the Bowery, he fell, apparently lifeless, to
the floor, in a manner worthy of a stage-actor.

This performance ended, a shout of applause
from his companions for a short time prevented any other sound from being audible, and
then little Lyons was called for.

A mite of a boy took the floor, to the very
evident delight of the company, who were well
acquainted with his powers of melody.

He stood a moment looking round on the audience, and then, in a clear, musical voice, sang a song, which was a recital of his own experience.

"My name is Paddy Lyons ; I'll sing a little song ;
And as I'm rather short myself, it wont be very long.
I make the news-boys merry ; and they sometimes take the hat,
And make a small collection for their funny little Pat.

" I have a scolding step-mother ; — she made her house too hot ;
So Paddy Beef cleared out in time ; but trouble was his lot ;
An M. P. put me out to board ; but soon I got away,
And in the baker's basket was carried out one day.

"Step-mother was a blessed one to get upon a spree :
She licked poor Paddy twice a day, as hard as hard could be ;
He had to wear her petticoat, and nusre her bawling Bob ;
I fetched her brandy for her nog, — she paid me on the nob.

" I showed my heels, and cut my stick, the shanty saw no more ;
I went up to the Bull's Head then, and sang before the door :
I sang for six fat butchers there, till they forgot their grief, —
They gave me half a dollar, and they called me Paddy Beef.

" If any friend should look for me, he wont have far to roam :
He'll find me at the Lodging-House, the news-boy's happy home,
There I'll be glad to stump a speech, or sing a merry song, —
And now I'll close my melody, before it gets too long."

When the song ceased, the boys raised a perfect storm of applause, and indulged in such characteristic demonstrations of delight, that it was deemed best to call them to order; and Paddy jumped from the stool on which he had been standing, with a bound that would have done credit to a monkey, and took his seat demurely.

In the intimacy which grew up between our two heroes, Jack narrated all the circumstances of his early life, the friendship which had grown up between his mother and the widow Holland, and also the kindness and generosity of Mr. Sennott toward himself. These names were afterwards so often repeated between them, that they became almost as familiar to one as to the other.

Edward Morris was tall and athletic for a boy of his years. His hair was of a raven blackness, and his cheeks dark and sunburnt, from long exposure to every variety of weather.

He was far from prepossessing in appearance ; and yet, when excited, there was a kindling up of the eye, and indeed of the whole face, which gave indications of genius.

Jack, on the contrary, was rather beneath the usual size. His hair was dark auburn, and he still continued to wear it long and waving on his forehead, as when his mother was alive. He was considerably freckled, but there was a singular fascination about his eye, which others beside Mr. Sennott had remarked. There was a depth of expression, an earnest longing for something not yet attained, which arrested the attention and stirred the heart of the beholder.

Both Edward and Jack were enterprising news-boys. Beside the small pittance daily paid for their privileges at the Lodging-House, they had quite a sum due them at the bank connected with the institution.

" Ned, come out here a minute ; I want to

4

talk with you," called out Jack, one evening, soon after they had reached the Lodging-House.

"I don't believe Edith Holland has enough to eat," he went on, when they were secure from interruption.

"You don't say so!" was the astonished rejoinder.

"Yes; that's it. You know I told you how thin and pale she was growing, and how sunken her eyes were, that used to be so beautiful."

"Yes."

"Well, to-night I ran in there to deliver a bundle, and they were eating supper. And do you think, Ned, only one slice of bread for the three. Then they had some weak, wish-washy looking stuff they called tea; but Edith didn't take any of that. She ate her bread, and then she looked at the others, watching every piece they put into their mouths, like a hungry dog. I tell you what it is, Ned, it's real mean of me

to come here and eat down a hearty supper,
and let a girl like Edith Holland go hungry to
bed; but I haven't told you all yet.

"When I came out into the entry I stopped
a moment, trying to get courage to go back
and give them what I had in my pocket. It
may seem easy enough to you, while we're sitting here; but they're ladies, no sham, but real
genuine ladies, though they are so poor; and
I know just what a look of astonishment the
old lady'd give me with her eye. While I
stood there I heard her say, 'Edith, you must
take your part of the tea. I didn't say anything before Jack; but I've saved it for you in
my cup.'

- "Then I heard Louisa saying, 'Oh, what
would Fred say, if he knew how Edith was —
how we were all suffering! Why will Uncle
Sears treat us so?'

"I don't know who these people are; I
never heard their names before; but I was all

chocked up, and bolted down the stairs as quick as my feet would carry me.

" But," exclaimed Edward, " you must manage somehow to carry them something. I will give you all I have ; for we can do without new clothes better than they can without bread."

Jack sprang to his feet, clapping his hands together with a noise that made the room ring.

" I'll tell you what it is, we'll go together," he cried. " Let's go now and get leave from Mr. Rogers."

" I'd ask him what to buy," suggested Ned.

" So we will, but don't mention their names.

It was near seven o'clock, on a cold, autumnal evening, that Mrs. Holland and her two daughters sat sewing by one dim candle, when they heard heavy steps coming up the stairs, and presently a vigorous knock at their own door.

CHAPTER IV.

"COME in," answered a low voice, belonging to Mrs. Holland.

To their surprise, their old friend Jack Stetson entered, accompanied by a youth whom he introduced as Edward Morris, the best fellow, and his most intimate friend at the Lodging-House.

Now Edward had doubted considerably whether Jack's descriptions of Edith's beauty were not greatly exaggerated ; but one glance into that face, pale and sunken though it was, convinced him that the half had not been told him. He stood, awkward and embarrassed,

53

twirling his cap in his hands, paying no heed
to the repeated invitations for him to take a
seat.

Jack was more at ease. Indeed, it was plain
to see that he had come with a purpose, and
was considerably excited in regard to its success. He began at once.

" How soon shall you want me to take that
bundle of work home ?"

The widow looked up somewhat surprised,
but answered, quietly, " It will last us a day
or two yet."

" I have brought some shirts, Edith," he
continued, more shyly; " will you make them
for me ?"

She looked up, and nodded her head, with a
smile that almost threw Edward out of his
chair.

" There's two for me and two for Ned," Jack
went on; " and we want 'em done up in first-
rate style. They're real Sunday, go-to-meeting

shirts, such as mother used to say my father wore ; and we expect to pay up high for making 'em.

You needn't hurry, either," he added, as he saw the widow make a sudden movement ; "only as we are flush in cash, we want to pay down in advance."

So saying, and before a word could be heard in reply, he laid down upon the table a bankbill, with the figure five stamped upon it.

" God be praised ! " ejaculated the poor woman, while her daughters cast such a glance of gratitude upon the young men, that they felt that they would willingly give another V to have it repeated.

" And now that's settled," Jack went on, "I want to ask a favor of you. If 'taint convenient, I hope you'll say so ; but you see it's a year now since mother died, right in that room yonder, and — well," he stammered, coloring painfully, " the fact is, Ned and me haven't

had a hot dinner for a long time, and we have
a kind of hankering after some beef soup and
apple dumplings."

Mrs. Holland grew very pale. She could
not understand that this was a contrived plan
to give the entire family one hearty meal without intruding on their delicacy ; and supposed
that the bank bill, for which she had so earnestly
thanked God, was to be appropriated to the
dinner. The fact that the landlord was to
come in a few hours for his rent, which, with
their utmost economy, they had not been able
to lay by, pressed with equal weight on the
minds of both mother and daughters. The
bank bill, which more than covered the amount
they owed him, had instantly been appropriated
to that most urgent necessity; but to talk of
apple dumplings and beef soup, it was too
tantalizing !

These thoughts darted through the mind
of the poor woman while Jack was speaking,

much quicker than I can write them ; and he,
noticing the sudden change in their appearance, seemed unable to conclude his sentence.
But at last, seeing Edith's large mournful eyes
fixed earnestly upon him, he burst out:

" The fact is, I've been and told Ned how
kind you was to mother, and how many little
jobs you've done for me ; and we thought
'twould do you all good to give up that ever-
lasting stitching for one day at least. We've
bought the beef and fixings ; but if you can't
conveniently ask us to eat dinner with you to-
morrow, we'll thank you just the same, won't
we, Ned ? "

" Yes, indeed ! " was the earnest response.

" Jack Stetson," said Louisa, with a smile,
though her eyes were twinkling with tears,
" you're the best little fellow in the city. We'll
have the dinner ready at any time you say,
and many thanks to both of you for your
kindness."

"That was done first-rate," cried Ned, when they were once more in the street, "I'll give Mr. Rogers the palm for planning; but my heart fails me when I think of sitting down to eat with that beautiful girl."

Jack laughed aloud and presently was joined by his companion. "Now for the grocer's," he said, heartily.

In less than an hour they were again at the widow's door; but this time accompanied by the grocer's clerk, bearing numerous small bundles of provisions, while Jack carried a bag of flour and meal and a huge sack of potatoes.

"How I wish your mother were alive to-night," murmured Edith softly, as they all stood near the door.

"To know that her prayers for her boy are being answered," added the widow.

"And that he has chosen such good companions," suggested Edith, looking with admiration in Edward's glowing face.

"I'll tell you what it is, Jack," remarked Ned, as, after having fixed the hour for the coming fête, they silently bent their steps toward the Lodging-House, "I mean to be a man, and worthy to be a companion to such women as we saw to-night. But would they have spoken so kindly to me if they knew what a vile fellow I was once?"

"Yes, Ned, that they would. All really good people try to help those who mean to reform. But wont Mr. Rogers be pleased at our success?"

As they entered the Lodging-House, they found that the school, which was usually in session at this hour, was dispersed, and Mr. Rogers engaged in examining a lad who had given him a great deal of trouble, and who had now been convicted of stealing.

The boys were standing around in groups, warmly discussing the probable fate of their companion, while a man with a star on his breast sat near the Superintendent patiently awaiting the result.

The officer, as well as the boys, knew that Mr. Rogers always inclined to clemency; and that he had in many instances rescued his scholars from imprisonment by becoming himself responsible for their good behavior. But this case was so flagrant an act of crime, and the offense had been so often repeated, that the good man feared the influence of such a determined thief might be of positive injury to his other boys.

Finding that the Superintendent would not be able to attend to their story, Edward and Jack found a quiet place in the school-room where they could talk over the anticipated pleasures of the morrow.

After a short time they noticed that the officer led the young thief away. Then came the call to prayers, after which all went orderly to their beds.

The next morning Jack was early at his business. He ran to the office of the Journal of Commerce, Ned having bent his steps to another part of the city, he being connected with a different paper. He had already sold more than half his papers, and was calling out in rather a more animated tone than usual, "Morning ede-shun, Journal o' Commerce," when he turned quickly, at a touch upon his shoulder, to see Mr. Sennott smilingly regarding him.

"Have a paper, sir?" inquired Jack, holding out his remaining numbers.

"Yes, I will. I bought one last evening, and found on opening it I had been cheated into taking one a day old, instead of an hour, as the lad professed."

Jack laughed. "Yes, sir, them are smart chaps; they buy the back papers dirt cheap, 'cause they're gone by, you see, and then they make quite a spec out of it."

"But Jack, I hope you have never so far forgotten your mother's instructions as to do that."

"No, sir. Ned and I have talked it all over, and we think it don't pay. You see, sir, gents as have been cheated once, look sharp next time ; so what them smart chaps make one day, they lose the next."

The attorney smiled. "Yes, that's it," he said. "I shall look sharp when I see that news-boy again. But, Jack, how are you getting on ; and who is Ned ?"

"Oh, he's a brick ! — I mean," he added, coloring, "he's Mr. Rogers's best boy. He and I are going to have a dinner-party to-day."

"A dinner-party ! Well, you are getting up in the world."

A bright smile broke out all over Jack's face. He had an idea, which was nothing less than to secure Mr. Sennott for a friend to Mrs. Holland. The gentleman lingered a moment while he sold a paper and received the coppers, and was turning away, when Jack asked, earnestly, " May I go to your office and tell you about it ? "

" Yes ; you'll find me in till two."

It seemed to our news-boy that he had never been more successful than on this particular morning. Every gentleman who passed seemed in want of a paper, so that his remaining bundle was soon disposed of. He glanced at the clock, and found he had still twenty minutes before he started for school ; so he determined to pay his visit to the attorney at once.

The gentleman well remembered the fair, pensive face which had peeped into the widow's room the first time he visited her ; and listened with increasing interest to the lad's simple story.

He was particularly pleased with the refinement and delicacy of feeling manifested by the boys in supplying the necessities of their distressed neighbors, and determined at once to make an addition to the bill of fare at the dinner-party, as Jack laughingly designated it.

This was to come off as soon after five as our news-boy could be dismissed from school. Unfortunately his mind was so absorbed in wondering what Ned would say to Edith, and what they would all say to him, that he failed in recitation, and was condemned to half an hour's study after school hours. This was a terrible punishment, as the poor lad's sorrowful countenance plainly showed. But there was no help for it; and at last even this long half hour came to an end.

CHAPTER V.

WHEN Jack reached the house where Mrs. Holland lived he found Edward waiting outside the door, and they proceeded directly up stairs. A few words served to explain his late appearance, and the sight of the happy faces moving so briskly round the table, speedily caused him to forget both his late punishment and the cause of it.

There was some little confusion in drawing around the well-spread board. First there were chairs to be borrowed, as neither the widow's low rocking-chair, nor Edith's stool would suffice on so important an occasion.

5   65

Then there was a question who should sit at the head and do the honors, which was finally settled by Mrs. Holland removing the platter of meat to a position before her own plate, while Louise helped to the soup, and Edith's turn came with the dumplings.

Few except that unhappy class in our community who spend day after day in the monotonous employment of sewing for slop-shops, can appreciate the unaffected enjoyment of these young persons, when the tedious routine of their life was so suddenly broken. Edith, in a more merry tone than had been heard from her lips for many a day, declared, "It seems like a fairy dream; but I hope it will not end until I have had a taste of the dinner."

"Which I have already had," laughingly replied her sister. "I was so hungry, I confess, I could not wait while Jack was sitting on the penitent-bench."

Ned's countenance was a strange commingling of shyness and delight. Never had he been so determined to be worthy of the name of man, as when on this eventful occasion he first found himself seated at table with a company of virtuous women. Sitting awkwardly on the very verge of his chair, which he modestly refused to draw nearer the table, the blushes dyed his bronzed cheeks to a deeper hue as the widow, unexpectedly to him, gave hearty thanks to her Heavenly Father, for having put it into the mind of these young friends to provide food for the hungry. She implored so earnestly the blessing of Heaven upon them, that the youth, entirely unused to such scenes, found himself scarcely able to control his emotions.

The dinner-party was not destined to pass without other incidents; for the beef soup was scarcely removed, and the plates, borrowed from a neighbor below, placed on the table for the dumplings, when a knock was heard at the door.

Jack quickly sprang to prevent any stranger from intruding, but started back on seeing a man with a basket of fruit, which he said Mr. Sennott had sent for the dinner-party. His scream of delight brought all parties to the door. Mrs. Holland alone retained presence of mind sufficient to ask the messenger into the room, while her daughters, assisted by Jack, removed from the basket first some fine bunches of grapes, then some luscious pears, and afterwards two neatly-tied parcels which were found to contain tea and sugar. These last were marked with a pencil, "For the friends of Jack and Edward."

The starts of surprise, the excited exclamations from one and another of the party, as these wonderful things came to light, the delight painted on every countenance, the vehement terms of gratitude to the donor, were, as Mr. Sennott's servant told him, well worth the whole bill.

Nor did the wonders end here. At a later hour, and when the abundant remains of the feast had been removed, Mr. Rogers announced himself, with a smile, and requested of Jack an introduction to his friends.

It will be remembered that the Superintendent planned this mode of supplying the immediate necessities of the widow; but he was far from wishing this fact to be known. Jack, however, in his excitement at the unexpected visit, stated all the circumstances, much to the confusion of Edward, who caught a glance of Edith's animated features, and blushed till he could scarcely see.

Mrs. Holland tried to articulate her thanks, but the gentleman stopped her at once, by saying:

" I am sure, madam, you must perceive that it is the boys, and I, as their friend, who should

be grateful ; for the society of well-educated
ladies will be of far greater advantage to them,
than anything they have it in their power to
do for you."

"Yes, indeed," urged Edward ; and then,
frightened at the sound of his own voice, he
stopped abruptly.

"You are very kind, sir," answered the
widow. "There was a time when we were
more happily situated ; and when it might
have been in our power effectually to aid you
in your good work. Now we have the will,
but scarcely the means for anything beyond
the mere keeping together of body and soul."

Her voice quivered, and for a moment ceased ;
but she presently added, "Because the kindness of these young friends has made this day
a holiday long to be remembered, it is not the
less certain that to-morrow we must return to
our ceaseless tasks. But we do not complain.
We know that though clouds and darkness

are around about Him, righteousness and
judgment inhabit the throne of our Father in
heaven. No doubt he chastens us in love, and
we, as dutiful children, must pray for the
spirit of meekness, cheerfully to endure whatever trials he sees fit to send upon us."

This was new language for one, at least, of
the company; and Edward Norris, as he gazed,
at the resigned countenance of the widow and
then glanced toward Edith, whose hands were
engaged upon one of Jack's new shirts, but
whose face reflected her mother's words, felt
that this was true religion — the religion of
the heart. For the first time in his life a silent
petition went up from his soul that he too
might love God, and serve him as these poor
women did.

Jack was equally, though differently affected
by the widow's words. They recalled days long
gone by, when one who now lay alone in a
pauper's grave, had discoursed in like manner;

and they revived and strengthened many res-
olutions made by the coffin and the tomb.
He thought of his mother's triumphant death,
and the blissful eternity upon which she had
entered ; and acknowledged that even in this
life she had her reward.

" We have great encouragement in our labor," Mr. Rogers added, after a pause. " One
boy came to me lately and deposited tempora-
rily in the bank one hundred dollars, which he
had earned since last spring. Several, after
getting a taste for study at our evening schools,
are determined to fit for college."

A sudden start and exclamation of surprise
from Jack interrupted the gentleman for a
moment. Then, with a smile, he went on.

" Another boy is trying to earn a farm of
his own, besides being the promised heir of
a wealthy farmer."

" Is that Sammy, who went in the last lot ?"
inquired Ned, timidly.

"Yes, and a noble man he will make. Here his energies were cramped for want of room. In the grand, glorious West he will have space to grow. That boy will make his mark, or I'm mistaken."

Seeing that the widow and her daughters were greatly interested, the Superintendent went on, "I have some letters in my pocket from boys in the West which I will read to you.

"Here is one from a lad who was homeless and friendless in the streets for a long time before he found his way to the Lodging-House:

"'DEAR SIR:—I have been thinking of writing to you for some time; but I have been so busy I could not. I think I ought to write to you twice a year, to let you know how I get along. How glad I am that when I was at the Lodging-House, I improved the opportunity of learning to write. If I had idled instead of studying, I could not now have had the pleasure of informing you that I attended school last' summer; and my kind friends with whom. I live have promised I should go through a regular course of study at an institution near this place. Sometimes in the night I wake all covered with sweat, dreaming I am back in the city, on the top of a hay barge or under a wagon, where I often used to lie, instead of being in a comfortable bed (real hair mattress) in my neat room at the farm.

"'I can scarcely yet realize the change that has come to me, and that by your kindness and that of good people who set up the Lodging-House, I have a beautiful home and friends who help me to be a good and useful man.

"'When I am out of school, I do chores about the farm; and there are enough of them, I tell you.

"'We have three hundred and fifteen hogs,

two hundred chickens, plenty of geese, — old geese and goslings, — and lots of pigeons. Sometimes I take Pinky, the old horse, and ride horseback to the Post Office, three miles from here. I just wish some of the Lodging-House boys could see me. They wouldn't be contented another minute till they were in the cars for the West.

"'I didn't expect to write so long a letter; but I thought you would be pleased to know that I like my place tip-top, and that I mean to act by your advice, and make the most of my advantages.

"'Every night I repeat the prayer I learned of you, and thank God that I am not a friend-less orphan in the city; but that he led me to the Lodging-House, by which means I am now enjoying every comfort.

"'Please give my love to all the boys that I knew.   Yours, affectionately,

MOSES TURNER.'

"I didn't think Moses could write so good a letter," exclaimed Jack, warmly. "I'm glad he's got so good a home."

"Here is another letter from little Dan Watson. You remember him, Edward, I think. He left just before Jack came. He has gone to live with a farmer in Michigan. When he was sent to us, his father had gone to sea, and his mother was miserably poor, living in a filthy basement. He writes:

"'DEAR MR. ROGERS: — I have been very well since I left the cars. I suppose Mr. —— told you how sick I was then. I am well now. I am out on a farm of about two hundred acres of land. I have to do a great many chores, for they have a great deal of cattle.

"'I get up very early in the morning to light the fire, then feed all the cows, pigs, horses, lambs, chickens, ducks, hens, and geese. I have to feed a wee-wee, small sow; and I saw a horned lamb. I asked the man that I lived with, if it was a horned pig. You know we can't be silent all the time. You know we must have a little fun once in a while. Now I know you will laugh at this letter, because it is written so bad. Please forgive me for writing so crooked.

"'The people that I live with are very kind to me. They have given me a horse and a hundred dollars for myself to keep. They bought me a pair of boots that cost seventeen shillings. I am going to school soon.

DANIEL WATSON.'"

"I should think such letters would make all the boys want to go out West," said Edith, her deep blue eyes beaming with interest.

"They do, indeed, have a great effect on them," answered the gentleman; "and so far we have had no difficulty in placing our boys. The friends of the Lodging-House have more than realized their anticipations of its usefulness. Many a lad, but for this benevolent institution, would now be in the city prisons; or, worse still, strolling the streets, a curse to society, and ruining their own souls by their vices instead of being in comfortable homes where, by the blessing of God, they may be trained to be useful and honored citizens."

This was an eventful evening in Jack's life. Mr. Rogers had never seen him so excited as when he went on to give a glowing description of Mr. Sennott's present; and the boy afterwards confessed that it was the proudest moment of his life when Edith, at a glance from her mother, arose and presented their guest with a plate of delicious fruit.

No one but he and Edith knew that the largest and ripest bunch of grapes had gone to the couch of a poor seamstress directly underneath them — one whose days were already numbered; and now to be one of a party to entertain their good Superintendent, it was almost too much honor for one evening.

It was still early when Mr. Rogers took his leave, after having invited the ladies to visit the Lodging-House, and the boys soon followed him, being eager to be by themselves and enjoy the dinner party anew by discussing its merits. Little did they suspect how quickly the extra candle was extinguished, while the widow and her daughters drew closer around the table, being eager to complete the four shirts, the generous pay for which had been already passed over to their landlord.

"What a happy day this has been!" said Louise, holding her needle closer to the light in order to thread it.

"Now it has passed, it seems more like a dream than ever," answered her sister.

"We have pretty substantial proof that it is not," remarked the widow, with her own patient smile. "There is provision enough to last us a long time."

"I feel stronger already," said Louise, "that

beef soup was so relishing;" and she moved her lips as if again enjoying it.

"I saw neither Edward nor Jack eat much," suggested Edith; "but I understood their motive."

"Do you think we said enough to thank them?" inquired the widow. "It must have cost them a great deal."

"I shouldn't wonder if they took every cent they had in the bank," rejoined Louise, "for the dinner and their shirts. I wonder whether all Mr. Rogers's boys turn out as well. I saw Edward shrank from being known in it at all; but we shall see them again, and can tell them how happy they have made us."

"The Superintendent said that he had many discouragements," remarked Mrs. Holland, "but was sure the lodging-houses would be a great blessing to the community."

For the next hour the girls chatted quite merrily at their work, and then Edith ran down to minister to the wants of their sick, almost dying neighbor, before she retired to her own humble bed.

In the mean time the widow sat silent and absorbed. The cares of life were settling heavily again on her heart.

She said to herself, "There are flour and meal, and a sack of potatoes, but no wood to cook them. The food already prepared will last a few days, and then, unless we can earn more than usual, we shall once more be in want."

She upbraided herself for the fears so natural to a mother, and tried to fasten her mind upon the promise of the Saviour, who, after stating his care for his children and his power to make all things work for their good, says, "Take therefore no thought for the morrow, for the morrow shall take thought for the things of itself; sufficient unto the day is the evil thereof."

6

When Edith returned from her labor of love,
the widow arose, and, laying aside her work,
called upon Louise to read a few verses,
and then she committed herself and her dear
daughters to the watchful care of their Heavenly Father, with a blessed assurance that he
would fulfil his promise toward them.

CHAPTER VI.

THE NEWS-BOY'S SPEECH.

IT was rather late the next evening as Jack entered the Lodging-House. When he was in the school-room one of the little fellows pulled him by the sleeve, and, with a sly wink, whispered, "There's a treat. Mind your manners, and you'll get a bite."

Jack laughed. He saw that something unusual was taking place, and had no sooner reached his seat near Edward than a gentleman arose to address them.

"I am glad to meet you," he began. "I was told that I should find something of interest at the News-Boy's Lodging-House; but I did not expect to be half so well pleased. I am a

83

stranger in the city. I live on a prairie farm in the great West."

'"Good! good! I'm going West," "I want to be a farmer," "I'll go back with you," was the loud, earnest cry from many voices.

"Last night, at ten o'clock, I met a news-boy. He was smaller than any of you except that little fellow [pointing to Paddy Lyons]. By the light of the street lamp I saw he looked weary and hungry; but he had a bundle of of papers under his arm, and he called out —

"'Evening ede-shun — News by the steamer — Latest extra. Want a paper, sir?' to every one who passed him.

"I was waiting for an omnibus, and I thought I would ask the little fellow why he did not go home. What do you think he answered?"

"Hadn't any home," cried one.

"Dad is dead and mammy's drunk," whined another, in a mimicking tone, which set the school into a roar.

"He had no father or mother; but there was a woman who sometimes let him sleep in her cellar, and she had forbidden him to go there till he had sold all his papers. He held up his bundle to show me that he had still quite a number, and faltered, pleadingly, 'I'll sell 'em cheap, sir, — dirt-cheap. Wont you take one?'

"My heart ached for the little news-boy, whose tearful eye reminded me of my own darlings at home; so I said, 'Count them, and I'll take them all.'

"He gave a scream of joy; and, tumbling the papers over, announced that there were thirteen. When I had paid him, to my great astonishment he turned a complete somerset on the pavement, crying —

"'Now I'll have some supper.' At that moment the omnibus came along, and I lost sight of him."

"Good! good! You're a keen one;"

" You 'll do," together with loud clapping of
hands, here interrupted the speaker.

" But I did not forget him. Even when I
was in bed I lay wondering where he was, and
wishing I could take him out to my farm,
where corn and wheat and potatoes are so
plenty, that no one need to go hungry."

" Take me — I'll go ; " " And I too," cried
one and another.

" I thought, too, that I should like to ed-
ucate that orphan boy, and see what he would
become in our great, growing country. I think
he was smart! I think all news-boys are
smart."

" So they are! That's the talk! "

" I feel confident that all news-boys need, is
an opportunity to do something, in order to
distinguish themselves. Suppose, for instance,
you, or you, little fellow, were to wake up to-
morrow morning and find yourself on a large
farm, where there were horses, and sheep, and

hundreds of acres of corn and wheat growing, and wild fowl to be had for the shooting; Suppose that you were treated kindly, as boys always should be treated; that you had enough to eat and drink and friends to be interested in your welfare; do you think you would steal from your master, or lie to him, or shirk your business?"

"No! no! no! That's what I wouldn't."

"No, no, no," I say. "You would love your new home; you would love your master and mistress; you would love the horses that you fed; you would love the sheep that came running at your call; you'd love the grand old trees waving over you; and by and by you'd begin to love your Heavenly Father, and thank him for sending you there."

Here there was such a tumult of applause that the gentleman sat down; but after a few moments rose again, and said, "I have not quite done. Your good Superintendent tells

me that there are a great many boys who
are sent to the West every year from the
Lodging-House, — that they like to go, — and
that he hears good accounts from them when
they get there. Now let me tell you that the
boy who is industrious and persevering in his
business here ; the boy who abstains from
swearing, from telling lies, from being low and
vulgar in his manners or conversation, is
the boy we want out West ; and when he gets
there, he's the one who rises to be a rich
man, a good neighbor, a Governor, perhaps.
But, on the other hand, the boy who steals,
and lies, and swears, and drinks rum, and
fights in the streets, is the one who ought to
stay in the city, where the police can take
care of him. We don't want him in the West.
We have no police officers on our farms or
near them."

"It's no great of a loss," said one. "Good
luck to you, sir," cried another. "Hurrah,

boys! Three cheers for the farmer from the West!"

And three such hearty cheers as they gave, some rising, some throwing up their arms, you seldom heard.

"Now," said the Superintendent, when he could be heard, "we have all listened to the gentleman's speech with great pleasure, and I want him to see that news-boys, too, are capable of making speeches. Who do you choose for your orator?"

"Paddy! Paddy!" shouted one and all. "Come out, Paddy. "Why don't you show yourself?"

Presently Paddy came forward, with a comic twinkle in his eye, and stood upon a stool. He was not more than twelve years of age, with a short nose, a small round eye, a lithe form, and his phiz chuck full of fun.

Looking round slowly, as if he were address-

ing a large audience, he began, in his own
peculiar style :

"Bummers, snoozers, and citizens, I've come
down here among ye to talk to ye a little. Me
and my friend," pointing to the gentleman from
the West, have come to see how ye're gitting
along and to advise yer. You fellers as stands
at the shops with yer noses over the railin's,
smellin' ov the roast-beef and the hash; you
feller who's got no home, think how good we
are to encourage ye!"

Ha ha's, and shouts of derisive laughter
here interrupted the speaker.

"I say, bummers, — for yer all bummers
[in a tone of kind patronage] ; I was a bum-
mer once [great laughter], — I hate to see
yer spendin' yer money on penny ice-creams.
Why don't you save yer money? You feller
without no boots, how would you like a new
pair — eh? Well, I hope you may get 'em;
but I rayther think you wont."

Here there was great laughter from all the boys except the one addressed.

"I have hopes for you all. I want you to grow up to be rich men, citizens, government-men, lawyers, generals, and influence men. Well, boys, I'll tell you a story. My dad was a hard 'un. One beautiful day he went on a spree; and he came home and told me 'Where's yer mother?' and I axed him I didn't know; and he hit me over the head with an iron pot, and knocked me down, and me mither drapped in on him, and at it they went."

Paddy was here interrupted with loud "Hi hi's," and demonstrative applause.

"Ah! at it they went; and at it they kept; — ye should have seen 'em — and whilst they were fightin' I slipped meself out the back door, and away I went like a scart dog."

"Come, now, dry up! Bag your head, Paddy. Simmer down."

"Well, boys, I wint on till I kim to the 'Home for the Friendless;' and they took me in and did for me, without a cap to me head or shoes to me feet, and thin I ran away, and here I am. Now, boys [with mock solemnity], be good; mind yer manners; copy me, and see what ye'll become."

As he made his bow, the youthful Demosthenes jumped from his stool, and was soon engaged in a dispute with a big boy who believed all that Paddy had said.

"Now," said Mr. Rogers, "you are invited to partake of some apples which our good friend the farmer from the West has provided."

"Good! good!" "That's delashus!" "He's the kind!" was the unanimous response; and presently huge pans of apples were brought in and passed around.

Soon after, a hymn was given out, which all joined heartily in singing, and then retired quietly to their beds.

CHAPTER VII.

JACK ASPIRING.

FOR several days Jack watched for the appearance of Mr. Sennott, with the double purpose of thanking him for his present and soliciting work from the ladies of the attorney's family. He had incidentally learned that both mother and daughters were qualified to engage in much more profitable employment ; and would be thankful for embroidering or dressmaking.

But he watched in vain. Neither in his office, nor at his residence in B—— Street, where the boy lingered on several successive mornings, could he see anything of the gentleman.

At length he mustered up resolution to inquire of the office clerk, and learned to his
dismay that his benefactor had gone with his
family to Europe for the benefit of his daughter's health.

This was a severe blow to the brilliant ex-
pectations he had formed of securing to Mrs.
Holland a powerful friend ; but in the busy
life he now led (he had been advanced to the
highest class in the school), one month after
another wore away until Christmas, with its
festivities, was at hand.

All honor to those benevolent persons who,
in the midst of their own happiness, do not
forget the friendless children at the lodging-
houses.

The occasion this year was a peculiarly
happy one. Christmas day, though cold, was
clear and bright. Contributions for the dinner began to arrive before the company of
news-boys started on their daily round, causing

loud bursts of merriment, with cries from the younger ones.

"Good! good!" "We'll have a high dinner to-day." "Hi! see that gobbler." "Come, now, be quiet, will you?" "I smell plum pudding."

It required some urging from the Superintendent before they could tear themselves away from the scene of so much interest; but they comforted themselves that the sooner they went, the sooner they could return; and at length ran merrily down the long flights of stairs into the street.

Many a news-boy, that morning, as he sold his papers, uttered a hearty "I wish you a merry Christmas, sir," or "I wish you a merry Christmas, lady," thinking, perhaps, that these very persons had contributed toward their merriment and happiness at the dinner-table.

"I wish I could get rid of just these two papers," said one little fellow, meeting his companion, as the morning wore on. "All sold out but these two; and they burn my fingers, I want to get rid of 'em so bad."

Jack Stetson at this moment happened to be passing, and, pitying the little fellow, who was very thinly clad, he said:

"Here, Bill, give them to me. I'll sell them for you, and give you the money when I go to dinner. There, off with you, and get warm."

The earnest glance of wonder and gratitude was enough to cheer Jack's heart, though not a word of thanks was spoken, as, after the boy passed the papers to his companion, he started on the run for the Lodging-House, his only home.

It seemed to Jack that even this trifling act of kindness received its reward; for in a short time he had disposed of all his papers, and was ready to follow to the Lodging-House.

He found Ned waiting for him at the door,

eager to relate the events of the morning and talk over anticipated pleasures. They proceeded together up the long flights until they reached the school-room, where most of the boys were gathered, trying to wait patiently their summons to dinner.

Many strangers were coming and going, some carrying away empty baskets which had been filled with turkeys, chickens, and pies; others bringing fresh supplies, accompanied by the wishes of the donors that this might be a happy Christmas to the news-boys; and still others coming to witness with their own eyes the delight of the children, some of whom, perhaps for the first time in their lives, were seated at a bountiful meal.

And now the long waited for summons is heard; and what a rush there is down stairs to the dining-hall! Mrs. Rogers, with her smiling face and her kind word for each, is here and there and everywhere; adding another dish of meat, and making room by a little crowding for an additional pie.

The little fellows make a rush for the table, every faculty wide awake and ready for action, — heads erect, eyes staring in wonder at the bounties before them, nostrils dilated snuffing the rich aroma, and mouths watering for the entertainment to commence.

Two gentlemen, friends of the institution, assisted Mr. Rogers in carving the meat, while half a score of ladies performed the part of waiters most gracefully. After thanks had been offered to the Giver of all good for this new token of his favor, the work of eating commenced in earnest. One little fellow, who had been but a few days rescued from the street, made remarks on the food which occasioned a shout of merriment. As he saw the huge turkeys, legs of ham, and roast beef, he exclaimed:

"How can we eat such big things? Where did they come from?"

It was not until the appetite of the children was partially allayed, that they had time to admire the room, which was tastefully trimmed with evergreen, looped up with bouquets of flowers.

Mr. Rogers, who seemed more than ever like a father, directed everything, quieting the children when they became too noisy, without causing them to feel that they were under restraint.

When the meal was concluded, several of the visitors made speeches; to which, at the suggestion of their teacher, some of the boys responded, thanking their friends in their own peculiar way for remembering them on this happy occasion. This exercise was followed by singing, in the midst of which a poor boy came in from the street with a pitiful story of destitution, which elicited the sympathy of all.

When the company had retired, the boys,

determined to make the most of their holiday,
returned to the school-room, where an hour or
two was passed in merry games, speeches, and
singing; and then, having joined in the evening devotions, retired quietly to their berths,
all agreeing that this was the happiest day they
had ever passed.

Jack was still a news-boy; but Ned had been
promoted to a place in the office of the paper
with which he had long been connected. Notice
had been taken of him by one of the editors,
and, after inquiries made of Mr. Rogers, he
was advanced to setting type; and thus one of
his early dreams was accomplished. With this
change in his prospects, young Norris was
removed to a regular boarding-house, where
a number of young men, similarly circum-
stanced, had their home. The evening school,
too, had to be given up; but Mr. Rogers, who
still remained his friend and adviser, reminded
him that Benjamin Franklin gained great

knowledge, by improving every spare moment in the cultivation of his mind.

Once or twice every week, Ned, with his friend Jack, passed the evening in Mrs. Holland's quiet room. She did not now occupy the one where we last saw her, but had removed to another house in the same block; where, subject to a more considerate landlord, she had more privileges for the same money, and was sure she should not, for want of that prompt payment which she sometimes found impossible, be turned at once into the street.

It had become the custom for the lads to read aloud to the widow and her daughters, while they diligently plied their needles — Edward furnishing the reading from the office, where he had obtained permission of his master to take any of the books. These visits were usually accompanied by some trifling token of remembrance. Sometimes Jack bought a loaf of bread, and Edward a pound of meat, or

they put their funds together to eke out the
rent when it was due.   All fear of offending
by their simple gifts was quite past now; for
the widow and her daughters had come to
understand how great a pleasure it was to the
lads to feel that hers was a kind of home to
which they had a claim; and here they were
sure to find friends who could sympathize both
in their trials and sorrows.

Mrs. Holland and her daughters were de-
lighted to hear anything of interest concerning
the Lodging-House, and the labors of the in-
defatigable Mr. Rogers.

One evening the boys entered her room in
great glee. " We've had a fine time to-night,"
said Jack.

" I can't help laughing to think how pleased
some of the little fellows looked," exclaimed
Ned.

" Do tell us about it," urged Edith.

" Well," said Jack, " I will; but it's a pretty

long story. You see Mr. ——, a rich gentleman in this city, heard that there were a good
many boys in the Lodging-House who were in
need of shoes; so what does he do but ask Mr.
Rogers to make out a list for him of the number and sizes that were needed. They came
to-day, nailed up in three great boxes — three
hundred dollars worth ; and there they stood in
the entry till after supper. We always have a
little time for fun then, and better fun I never
wish to see than we had to-night. We were
all in the midst of a noisy game, when Mr.
Rogers brought down his hand on his desk,
and called us to order. The boxes had been
brought in, and the shoes lay on the large
table. I saw some of those little barefooted
fellows gazing wistfully at them.

"'Boys,' said Mr. Rogers, 'I want your
attention a few minutes.'

"'All right, sir' was the general response.

"'A kind friend has sent these shoes here

for those who have none. All·who need shoes
may raise their hands."

"Such a laughing and clapping of hands,
and crying 'Good! good!' 'I need some,'
'And I,' you never heard. One little fellow
began to cry, he was so glad. His feet were
all covered with chilblains, so that he had to
wear soft rags around them.

"Then they began to go up one at a time,
to have a pair fitted to their feet, and go back
to make room for the next.

"'Did you see that red-headed chap?' asked
Ned, laughing; 'how afraid he was that the
shoes would all be gone before it came his
turn. He tried to push little Paddy Lyons out
of the way, till Mr. Rogers said, 'Be patient,
Miles; your turn will come in time."'

"I know what I would do, if I were rich,"
exclaimed Jack. "I would spend all my time
going round among poor people and lodging-
houses, and making them happy."

"I think Mr. —— must be a happy man to-night," faltered Mrs. Holland, with glistening eyes. "Such men are an honor to humanity. We ought to thank God for them."

"If every rich man was like him," suggested Edith, "there would be very little suffering among the poor compared with the present."

She sighed; and Jack thought he saw a tear drop on her work.

"Well, I guess some of our chaps will go to bed with lighter hearts to-night," he said, in a cheerful tone, hoping to change the subject.

"Even if they have heavy heels," retorted Louise, laughing.

"I should like to have been there," said Edith, glancing up from her work.

"You have never accepted Mr. Rogers's invitation," exclaimed Jack, springing to his feet. "Why can't you go to-night?"

Mrs. Holland saw the color deepen in the checks of her daughters, and sighed as she felt obliged to deny this slight indulgence. But stern necessity was upon her, bearing her down with his iron grasp; and though she realized what a relief it would be for them to vary their monotonous toil by a visit to the Lodging-House, she said, calmly:

"Not to-night, Jack. We have promised that these shirts shall be finished."

Before they left, however, the boys succeeded in persuading them to name a day for the visit, Louise declaring that she would get up an hour or two earlier to earn the time.

CHAPTER VIII.

PERHAPS my young readers would like to accompany Mrs. Holland and her daughters on the visit proposed at the close of the last chapter.

Imagine yourself, then, at the top of a long flight, or rather of five flights of stairs, leading up through a dark passage to the door of a large apartment. In this, the rows of benches with the platform on each end indicate it as the school-room, play-room, and chapel.

Mrs. Rogers came forward, the sleeves of her dress rolled up above the elbow, and cordially greeted her visitors, whom Jack introduced as

107

his particular friends. Ned, who was also a
visitor, playfully seated them in the chairs set
apart for company; while Jack mounted the
platform, and gave them a speech.

Only two or three boys were to be seen
about, the rest being absent at their daily toil.
One of these, as ragged and dirty a little fellow as you would care to see, Louise at once
made a hero of, on account of his large, ex-
pressive eyes. She inquired of Mrs. Rogers
who he was, and where he would be likely to
be sent.

Going from this room, by another passage,
down one flight, they reached the lodging-
room, designed to accommodate about three
hundred. This apartment, with its neat patch-
work-covered berths, much interested the
ladies. The room was divided off by iron
posts, to which the tiers of berths were fastened
—the beds being made of stout wires, fastened
across from one post to another. Upon these

the wooden slats were placed, which were covered with nice little mattresses. Between every row of these berths was an open space, about two feet in width, so that they could be easily made up. Each one of them was numbered, as was also the lock-closet, allowed each child for the use of his clothes. The same number given to the boy's berth, was also given to his box in the savings bank, to his hook in the hall, and to his seat at the table.

Before they left this room, Mrs. Rogers informed them that, though a good deal of liberty was allowed the boys in the school-room and at their meals, here perfect order and quiet were enforced — no child being allowed to communicate at all, even with his nearest neighbor.

Adjoining the lodging-room was the eating-hall, with four rows of narrow tables. These were set for the next meal, which was supper, with plates of common earthen ware — a bri-

tannia cup, knife, fork, and spoon being given
to each child.

The fare, the matron informed them, was
wholesome and abundant, though exceedingly
plain. When rice was given them, it formed
nearly the entire meal. Hasty-pudding was a
favorite dish; and the diet was varied with
bread, hash, etc.

The next object of interest was the bank,
into which the boys were encouraged to put all
their savings. This was merely an immense
table, checked off into squares, which were
numbered. By the side of each figure was a
slit, or hole, through which the coin could be
dropped into the box beneath. The first of
every month the bank is opened, and every boy
who wishes can withdraw his money, or receive the interest on his deposit. The boxes,
with numbers corresponding to those on the
top, can be drawn out, so that each boy can
take his money.

While they were examining the bank, the Superintendent came in. After expressing his pleasure at seeing them there, he told them of an act of charity performed by a gentleman to the institution. A deposit of money was placed in his hands, to be loaned in small sums of twenty-five cents each, to such boys as were needy, to start them in business. Upon this deposit between four and five hundred dollars had already been made by the borrowers; which showed how many boys only need a little assistance at starting, in order to be able to support themselves. He said the cases were very rare where the borrowed money was not returned, though sometimes after the expiration of a month.

It was an incalculable benefit to Jack and Ned to have the acquaintance of such a family as Mrs. Holland's. Happy would it be if more of our youth could look forward to a quiet, profitable evening with those who have the fear

of God before their eyes, and who let their light
shine. In this instance, the benefit was mutual.

"Do you think the boys will come to-night?"
or, "This is the evening for Jack and Ned,"
were common words, as the day began to decline.

The future welfare of the lads was also a
source of much speculation. Louise prophe-
sied that Jack would be the most successful
man. But Edith had grown to understand
that her sister, on one point, did not always
speak her mind, and therefore made a point of
differing from her. Jack, however, as their
oldest friend, was very dear to them both.
During the year he had grown both taller and
stouter; and there was an appearance of talent
about him which won him many friends. Of
late they had noticed a change in his demeanor,
— not as if he was envious of his friend's
prosperity, but a growing dissatisfaction with
his own employment.

"It is well enough for a boy," he said, one evening; "but I have outgrown it. I am ashamed of myself every time I 'take out a bundle of papers."

"But you make a good business of it," responded Edward; "and since you have been able to buy so many at such a discount, and can so readily dispose of all you wish to the smaller boys, you seldom appear in the trade at all."

"No," cried Louise, laughing. "You are no longer a news-boy; you are a commission merchant."

To their astonishment he scarcely smiled. "I am sick of it," he said. "I want to be something better than a news-boy."

And this was true. What step to take, or in what manner to advance his position, he knew not; but this advancement was the subject of his thoughts by day, and of his dreams by night. Several times he talked with Mr. ●

Rogers, when one boy after another left the Lodging-House, having entered on some new employment, either in or out of the city. On several occasions when a number of the lads were sent out to the West to work on farms, he had expressed his wish to join them, and found it very hard to practise the virtue of patience, which the Superintendent was so fond of preaching. He was little aware that for several months his kind friend had been actively engaged in searching for some suitable opening for the lad, whom he considered a youth of uncommon abilities. No, he became moody under deferred hope, and had come to the determination to do something for himself, when two events occurred which, for the time, changed the current of his thoughts.

He was one morning distributing his papers to the tribe of boys he now employed, when he saw a gentleman approaching, in whom, after one quick, searching glance, he recognized Mr. Sennott.

With a glad bound he was by his side; and, forgetting how a year had changed his own appearance, eagerly spoke his words of " Welcome home, sir ! "

It was a full moment before the reply came ; and Jack, wounded to the core at this apparent coolness, was about to turn away, when the interrogation came, " Can it be possible this is my old friend Jack Stetson ? Why, you are very much grown, — and improved, I was going to add ; but of that I am not certain as yet."

The youth had now time to notice that Mr. Sennott wore a weed on his hat, and that he looked pale and careworn. " I am very glad to see you home again," he repeated, in a more subdued tone.

" And are you still at your old business, Jack ? " .

The news-boy colored painfully, as he answered, "Yes, sir; but I'm too old for it, and I intend to leave it."

"Well, you must come to my office soon, and tell me all your plans."

The gentleman sighed as he added, "I have met with a sad loss since I saw you. We buried our dear Alice at Nice."

There was a moment's pause, and then Jack asked, "How is Alfred, sir?"

Mr. Sennott's face lighted again. "Ah!" he responded, "Alfred is wonderfully grown — almost as large as you are. The voyage over set him up at once, and he has been growing hearty ever since."

"You must come and see him," the gentleman was going to add, but he checked himself. He was not quite sure how the news-boy had spent his time during the past year; and, therefore, whether he would be a proper associate for his boy. Besides, Alfred's tastes had rather changed since the day he had thrust his hand into that of the desolate orphan.

But could he have understood the influence the widow Holland and her two lovely, amiable daughters had exerted over the mind of the youth, he would have said, " Come! "

Only the next evening, and while our hero was debating the question with himself how soon it would do to intrude upon his benefactor, he called alone at Mrs. Holland's room to tell her the good news.

To his surprise Edith, as soon as he entered, arose and went into the adjoining apartment. Her eyes were swollen with weeping, and he could see the traces of agitation on the countenances of both Louise and her mother. The widow hastened to apologize for Edith's abrupt departure, by saying, " We have to-day seen a notice of the death of a gentleman — a relative. We were entirely unprepared for the event, and Edith is quite overcome by it."

Jack briefly expressed his sympathy, and then went on to tell his own news, noticing that while he did so Mrs. Holland followed her daughter from the room.

"Wasn't it singular?" asked Louise, after an anxious glance toward the door; "mother went to the store for a piece of calico, and when she came home this paper was wrapped around it. I took it up to read, and threw it down again; but Edith's eye fell upon this notice."

She pointed to a paragraph among the deaths, which Jack read with interest:

"Joseph Sears, of this city, aged sixty-one."

"He was my uncle," added the girl, speaking low, "and once the partner of my father."

Jack suddenly remembered the words he had heard! "O, Uncle Sears! how can you treat us so?" and asked, abruptly, "Was he a good man?"

"Hush!" she said, growing pale, "It is not

right to blame the dead ; beside, he may have repented, and become good before he died."

" But this paper is a month or two old," continued Jack. " I remember reading this article," pointing once to her notice, " a long time ago."

" Are you sure of it ? " she asked, eagerly, stretching out her hand for the paper, and becoming very much excited.

The top was torn off, and so they had not known the name of the paper ; but Jack told her it was the Commercial Advertiser ; and, turning to the last corner, his statement was confirmed.

With an exclamation of distress she ran to announce this fact to her mother ; and then the youth heard renewed sobs. He took his cap from the table, and was about to go away, when the door opened, and Edith entered. Her eyes were strained, and her whole appear-

ance wild, as she hurriedly asked, " Do you
say Uncle Sears has been dead so long ? and
Fred has not been to comfort us ! "

" Edith, dear child," gasped the widow, trying to hold her daughter's hand, " Jack may
be mistaken ; and if not, there are a thousand
reasons for his delay. You must continue to
trust him. You know — we all know — what
a noble man he is, and how incapable of be-
traying our confidence."

" But a whole month, mother ! " The voice
was agony.

" Well, my dear child, a month is not too
long to trust him."

" But it will break my heart, mother ! I was
so sure he would come at once. I had begun
already to expect him. But a month, — O
Fred ! "

" Poor Edith ! " murmured Jack to himself,
as, having silently taken his leave, he went
softly down the stairs. " If this Fred, whoever

he is, has played her false, he is a black-hearted villain."

The affection Edith had so long and effectually concealed, but now in her agony made known —speculation upon the circumstances attending her uncle's death, and wonder whether they would admit him more fully into their confidence, were themes for thought enough for one night; so that he did not, as usual, lie awake dreaming about the future, and building castles in the air for himself.   His dreams of success that night were for Edith.   He even forgot that Mr. Sennott had returned.

CHAPTER IX.

JACK AND THE ATTORNEY.

IT was several days before Jack sought an interview with the attorney; which interview, nevertheless, had assumed such importance in his eyes that he was exceedingly nervous as he mounted the stairs to Mr. Sennott's office.

Though his daily income from the papers was greater than it had ever been, he was no less fully resolved to leave the business, and do anything, however menial, if it would lead on to a higher station. During the last few days he had recalled to mind circumstances in the life of one and another of those who had after-

wards been distinguished, useful men ; and reflected with pleasure that many of them had
been reduced to greater distress than he ever
was, but, by persevering industry and energy,
had risen to a high rank in society. He
smiled, sometimes, when he thought how
closely his benefactor was connected with all
these visions of future greatness.

Mr. Sennott was to be the one who would
set up the ladder upon which he, Jack Stetson,
was to climb, step by step. Mr. Sennott was
the man who, in after years, would point him
out to his fellow-citizens and say, ".Here is
one whom I first knew as a news-boy. I am
proud to say I helped shape his course, and
encouraged him to set his standard high. Gentlemen, I have the honor to introduce to you
Hon. John Stetson, your Senator."

At such times Jack would draw up his form
to its full height, while his chest expanded and
his nostrils dilated with the pleasing anticipa-

tions. "I know I have powers," he frequently exclaimed. "I thank God for them. Sometimes when I am talking with Ned, dear fellow as he is, I feel convinced I have capabilities to rise above him. Overjoyed as he is with his present success, he aspires no farther; while I — I never can be satisfied till I have reached the highest social position."

But we must follow our hero into the attorney's office, where he found the clerk examining a bundle of papers tied with red tape, his pen stuck behind his ear, and his brow knit with anxiety.

"Is Mr. Sennott in?" the lad asked, timidly.

The clerk, without raising his eyes from the papers, said, "No." But just as the news-boy was turning from the room, he added, "In at nine."

As the clock on a neighboring spire showed that it was within a few minutes of that time, Jack concluded to wait outside the door.

His heart began to beat very fast. He wished that the clerk would go away, that he could unburden his troubles to his early friend. He meant to tell him how the past year had been spent, and what hopes, what aspirations had arisen in his breast.

The morning was quite cool ; and Jack, as he buttoned closer his coat, which Mrs. Holland had recently repaired for him, wondered that a rich gentleman like the lawyer did not have a brighter fire; for, being naturally neat and orderly, he had noticed that the ashes and cinders had not yet been removed, and therefore that the fire in the open grate burned but dimly.

While he was still speculating on this subject, a boy near his own age came whistling up the stairs. His hair was long and tangled, while a little cloth cap, soiled and faded from constant use, was set jauntily on the top of his head. This lad stared at Jack as he passed, and then went carelessly into the office.

Mr. Sennott almost immediately followed him. He gave his hand kindly to the lad, who only said, "I was waiting for you, sir;" and then they entered the office together.

The room was full of dust from the ashes which the lad was shovelling up and carelessly throwing into the hod. As soon as he could speak, for coughing, the gentleman exclaimed, angrily, "Stop that, you careless fellow! How is it that you are taking up ashes now, when your fire ought to have been made two hours ago?"

"Can't help making dirt, there's such a lot of cinders," answered the boy, in anything but a respectful tone — beginning again to shovel them up.

"You've been on a spree again," muttered the clerk, dryly, as he also began to cough.

The lad darted an angry glance towards the desk, but then formed his lips for a tune, and whistled one or two notes.

"How dare you?" exclaimed the lawyer, advancing quickly to the boy. "Leave the office at once, and don't let me see your face here again."

He took out his pocket-book, paid the lad some silver, and then motioned him to the door.

"If you and the clerk will please go out, I will have the grate cleared and swept in ten minutes," cried Jack, much pleased to have it in his power to do his benefactor a favor.

"I'm on my way to consult Tenny about that claim," said the clerk, taking his hat from a hook.

Mr. Sennott glanced at the desk, with the pigeon-holes stuck full of papers, involving estates worth thousands of dollars, and then at Jack, whose earnest eyes calmly met his, and without hesitation answered:

"Well, Jack, you shall have it your own way. I'll step down to the office while you have a chance to brush us up a little. That scamp of a fellow has tried my patience long enough."

The first thing Jack did was to take from a pile of old papers enough to open and spread over the desk, table, and sofa, then he went vigorously to work at the cinders; and in a short time, by dint of poking and blowing and sticking in pieces of dry kindling he found in the closet, he had a cheerful fire.

He then applied the broom vigorously to the carpet, which appeared as if it had not been swept for months; took up the dirt on a paper (he could not find the dust-pan), and then stood still to catch his breath while the dust was settling.

Before the papers were removed, Mr. Sennott returned, and glanced around the room with a smile.

"Ah! he said, "you have been making thorough work of it, I see."

"I should like to make your fire every

morning, sir," exclaimed the youth, his heart beating so he could hear it. "I should have the room ready for you at seven, instead of nine."

"A capital arrangement for me, Jack, but how could you sell your papers?"

"I am determined to give up being a news-boy, sir. I want to be getting up in the world."

The gentleman grew more interested. "But how would making my fire advance you? Explain that."

Jack colored, and hesitated. How could he tell the gentleman that he expected him to point out the path to future greatness?

"I am willing to do anything honest for a living," at length he went on ; "but I must have something to look forward to. I am tired of being nothing but a news-boy ; beside, Mr. Rogers says I am capable of keeping accounts, or of — "

9

"What should you like to be, if you could have your choice?"

"An honest politician," frankly answered the boy, remembering how well the name, 'Hon. John Stetson,' had suited his fancy.

The lawyer laughed heartily, as he exclaimed, "That would certainly be a new thing on the face of the earth."

"But, Mr. Sennott, isn't it possible for a man to be a good Christian and at the same time to love and serve his country?"

Instead of answering, the gentleman sat and thought while the youth carefully removed the papers, and shook them in the entry; then, finding a piece of cloth in the closet, proceeded to wipe the dust which had settled on the furniture. He did his work thoroughly, as if his whole heart was in it; and yet the gentleman saw the color come and go on his cheek.

"He that is faithful in that which is least, is faithful also is much," was the passage which flashed upon his mind, as he compared this youth with the one who had just been discharged. Then his thoughts went back to the death scene of the mother — how entirely she had trusted her beloved son to the protecting care of her God; and he asked himself, " Have I not a duty toward this lad, whom Providence has so repeatedly thrown in my way? " He started to see Jack's eyes fixed earnestly upon him.

" I have been wanting to talk with you, sir," the youth began. " I have waited a year for your advice."

Mr. Sennott looked at his watch, and said, " Caswell will be away an hour; " and then motioned Jack to a seat.

I need not repeat what the youth told his benefactor. It is sufficient to say that when the clerk returned, the lawyer had become deeply interested in his protégé, and felt confident that the ardent aspirations to which he had listened were not destined to be disappointed.

Not even to Ned, whom he felt could not appreciate it, had Jack ever laid open his heart with all its high aims, as he now had to this Christian attorney; and he felt convinced he had not spoken in vain.

"This is an age of improvement," said the clerk, in his dry, hard voice, after running his finger along the edge of the desk.

"I think none of your papers are disturbed, sir," suggested Jack. "I covered them carefully before I swept."

"Oh!" was the answer, with a comical smile.

The lad glanced at Mr. Sennott, who stood near the window, and then put on his outer coat. "I will be here to-morrow morning to make the fire, sir," he said; "but where shall I find the key?"

"At my house. Do you know where that is?"

" Oh, yes, sir. Is there a dust-pan, sir ? "

" I don't know ; but we will have all things in order in a day or two. Don't fail to come here to-morrow at twelve. I shall want to talk with you then."

Our hero ran down stairs, and some distance on the street, before he knew where he was going. It was now half-past ten, and he had not once thought of his school. Study seemed quite distasteful to him. He wanted to think, to dream. But, after standing a moment hesitating whether to take his place in his class or stroll down to the Lodging-House, he decided upon the former, and resolutely bent his steps to the school-room.

CHAPTER X.

THE next morning, just as the clock struck seven, Mr. Caswell entered the office. The fire burned and crackled in the grate; everything about the room was neat and in its place. Jack was folding the last newspaper, which he returned to the pile, and then, merely bowing, he took his cap and ran to distribute his papers. He found a group of boys impatiently waiting for him, and soon sent them to their daily tasks. Then he hastened down the street to take a peep at Edward, whom he had not seen for two days.

Twelve o'clock found him dismissed from

school, and once more at Mr. Sennott's office, where, to his delight, he found the gentleman alone.

"I have not forgotten you," was the lawyer's answer to his eager, inquiring glance. "I have been to see Mr. Rogers, as perhaps he told you ; and he approves of a proposal I am about to make you."

The youth gazed at the lawyer, his whole soul in his eyes. He tried to speak, but the words choked him. He realized that this was perhaps the crisis in his life.

"Mr. Rogers is a firm friend of yours," the gentleman went on. "He says you will succeed, because you are determined to succeed; and though what I have to offer you will not be much in advance of your present position, yet it may open the way for greater good. But first let me see how well you can write." He drew a sheet of paper forward, and, pointing to the pen and ink, said, "Copy that."

A few lines were written in a miserable, almost illegible hand, at the top of a sheet. Jack thought it was the commencement of a deed; but, whatever it was, he set himself resolutely to work to copy it.

"Capital!" exclaimed the gentleman, presently, taking the paper. "I wish I could write as legibly. Now I wish to say that Mr. Caswell is obliged to go away to-morrow, on business which will detain him a fortnight — perhaps longer. You may come here, take care of the office, copy letters, or do anything else of the kind which may come-up, for which I will pay you a small sum, — filling up your time with your studies as heretofore. By the way, have you ever begun Latin?"

"I can read a little, sir."

"That is fortunate. How should you like to go to college?"

Jack's countenance fairly shone. "If I

thought it was possible," he said, " I would
work night and day."

The gentleman nodded his head approvingly.
" No doubt," he replied, " if you improve your
time you will succeed admirably. The first
thing to be considered is a boarding-place."

" I know of one," suggested Jack, " where
Edward Norris boards."

" You may go this afternoon and secure a
place there. I suppose you will wish to notify
your old employers that you intend to leave
them; or supply your place by another. One
question before you go. Is that your best
suit ? "

" No, sir ; I have one which I wear on
Sunday."

The gentleman opened his pocket-book and
took out several bills. " You can buy another
suit, then. I shall wish my second clerk to be
dressed like a gentleman."

Poor Jack blushed crimson. " I can put on

my best clothes," he stammered. " I should prefer to wait, sir, until I have earned them."

" Pshaw ! " muttered Mr. Sennott, replacing the money. Nevertheless, he liked the lad's spirit.

Edward Norris was overjoyed that at last Jack's genius had been appreciated. " I always knew it would be so," he repeated again and again. " I shouldn't be at all surprised if you came to be editor of a paper." This was to Edward the height of ambition.

From the printing-office Jack went to the boarding-place ; but was sadly disappointed to find the house completely filled. He expressed so much regret at not being with his friend, that the landlady at length told him she could give him his meals, if he would find a bed at the Lodging-House. He was just about to accept this proposition, when he recollected he was not now his own master, and that he ought to consult the lawyer. He engaged the place, therefore, and agreed upon the price conditionally, promising to come the next day to dinner if possible.

He had not seen Mrs. Holland for several days, being told by Louise when he went to the door that poor, dear Edith was sick. He resolved now to go and inquire for her. Seeing some fine-looking apples in the market, he bought a few, put them in a paper bag, and walked rapidly toward the house. He sincerely hoped Edith would be better, both for her own sake and for his. He felt it to be absolutely necessary for him to have some one to whom he could impart his joy.

He put out his hand to knock at the familiar door, when he was startled to hear a manly voice in earnest conversation. He hesitated a moment whether to go in, and then gave a timid knock.

Louise came quickly, and in a voice half way

between a laugh and a cry exclaimed, "O
Jack! come in, — we are all so happy!"

The youth did not doubt it when he entered.
Edith was sitting on her stool, indeed; but a
gentleman was close by her side, his eyes
resting fondly on hers, while her whole countenance fairly beamed with joy.

The widow stood before them, her hand
raised in earnest reply to what he, the gentleman, had said. She smilingly welcomed their
old friend, and Edith cordially extended her
hand. "This is our good, kind Jack," she said,
"who has helped us through so many troubles.
And this," she added, turning to the lad, "is
Mr. Sears."

"No, it's cousin Fred," cried Louise, laughing in an excited manner. "Jack knows who
cousin Fred is."

The youth bowed, wondering whether Mr.
Sears knew he had been a news-boy.

"Come this way," added the young girl,

" and I'll tell you all about it. It's the funniest thing you ever knew."

They sat together at the farther end of the room, while she narrated the few facts she had heard from her cousin.

Mr. Joseph Sears, her uncle, had died, as Jack had said, two months before. His son was travelling in a distant state, and, not receiving the intelligence, did not reach home until a fornight previous to this time. He found important letters from his father, both to him and to the wife of his former partner. They did not yet know the contents. Frederick immediately began a search for his relatives. One whole week he had passed in Baltimore, where he learned they had once been seen. At last he returned to New York, determined to advertise. He went to the office of the Commercial Advertiser; and it so happened that Edward Norris heard the name of Holland, and learned that the gentleman was

in search of his relatives. He approached the
desk where Mr. Sears was talking with the
gentleman, and said he knew a Mrs. Holland
who had two daughters.

"Named Edith and Louise?" was the quick
interrogation.

"Yes."

"Tell me where they live, and it shall be
money in your pocket," exclaimed the gentleman.

The direction was quickly given, and in a
few minutes Fred knocked at his aunt's door,
and had his own betrothed bride in his arms
once more.

Jack's eager countenance showed that he
sympathized in her joy.

"He says we have done with slop-work forever," gayly added the young girl. "He wants
to be married immediately, and then mother
and I shall live with them in Uncle Sears's
house. I don't know how they will manage

it. But just look at Edith, — isn't she happy?"

"I never saw her look so handsome," murmured Jack, softly.

"I have something I must tell you before I go," he added. "I know you will be glad, though you have so much that is pleasant to think of."

"Yes, indeed ; we shall always love you Jack. Edith told Fred what a good friend you have always been ; and you know if you had not brought Ned here, Fred might never have found us. So we owe all our good fortune to you."

"Under God," added the widow, solemnly.

"I have given up my old business of selling papers," Jack went on, rather proudly. "I am clerk in Mr. Sennott's office ; and I'm going to college ; and I intend to be somebody some time."

Louise bounded up from her seat. "Good !

good!" she exclaimed. "This is a happy day indeed. I must tell you, Edith, Jack's going to college. Jack's getting up in the world; and so am I. Oh, I shall be glad if I'm not crazy with all this joy!"

Both Mrs. Holland and Edith heartily responded to this welcome intelligence, and Mr. Sears grasped Jack's hand in a manner that said a great deal.

On leaving his friends, Jack was making his way toward the Lodging-House, when he encountered Mr. Sennott and his son Alfred. The latter had grown so much that he did not at first recognize him; and indeed when he did, he thought him not improved by his travels. The youth was dressed in Parisian style, and had a tiny cane in his hand, with which he continually whipped the air. He spoke to Jack in an off-hand way, as if it was rather a condescension to notice him.

His father, however, made up for his want

of cordiality. He asked Jack whether he had been successful in finding a boarding-place, and thus the lad had an opportunity to learn his wishes concerning the Lodging-House.

"Certainly, there is no objection to your remaining there for a short period," he said, after a moment's thought; "but you ought to have a good home."

10

CHAPTER XI.

AFTER he left Mr. Sennott, Jack made his way toward the Lodging-House, determined as soon as he had eaten supper to make a call on Ned, whom he missed exceedingly now that he needed some one to whom he could confide his plans for the future. He walked slowly on, building airy castles of success: fame, honor, riches seemed almost within his grasp. He would work hard, and render himself so indispensable to his employer that he would not be willing to part with him for a long time.

The boys were in the hall eating supper

146

when he entered; and before they rose, the Superintendent announced that he had some letters from his boys at the West, which he would read to them after their hour for recreation.

This was always a pleasant occasion, eagerly anticipated by the lads; and during their games they continually reverted to the expected treat.

"I wonder whether we shall hear from Jim Bunting?" said one.

"Or Patrick McMullen?" said another. "His'll be the funny letter, I'll be bound."

"Boys," commenced Mr. Rogers, "the first letter I shall read you is from our old friend Sammy J——. Many of you know him well. He says:

"'My Dear Teacher, and Fellow Pupils: I think by this time you will be pleased to hear again from me; and so I take my pen to write you an account of myself and my new

home. . I wish instead of writing I could
mount the stool little Paddy used to stand on
and talk to you. I guess I could make you
laugh at some of my funny adventures. When
I first came out here, I had never seen a cow
milked .in my life ; but I was ashamed to say
so, and they all took it for granted that I was
first-rate at the business. I followed Mr. L——
to the barnyard the first night after I arrived,
and watched with all my eyes. " That's easy
enough," I said to myself. " I can squeeze
milk out that way on the run."

" ' The next morning I got up early, and,
taking a mug from the kitchen closet, thought
I would try .my luck before anybody was
awake. Now it's very important to go up behind a cow on the right-hand side when you
are going to milk; but I didn't know this
then, and it happened that I went up on the
left side. I hung the handle on two fingers,
and had already got it half full, when the cow

gave a sudden kick at the mug, and to my astonishment left nothing of it but the handle in my hand for me to look at.

" ' I was very angry, and drew back my foot to give the ill-natured creature a kick, when I heard Mr. L——'s voice, ha-haing with all his might.   He had seen the whole from the barn window ; and I had to confess to him that milking was new business to me.

" ' The next day Mr. L—— heard me sing‚ ing ; and he told me mooly would like to hear me sing while I was milking, and that if I did she would soon let me milk her as well as she did him.

" ' I am going to learn to plough, and I expect to be a great farmer.   Mrs. L—— and her daughters are very kind to me.   They say that they love me like a child.   They like to hear me tell about the Lodging-House, and sometimes I make a speech to them as I used to there.

" 'Though I am so pleasantly situated, I do not forget your kindness, nor my promise to the boys to look out a place for them. I wish every poor city boy could come out here, where there is enough to do, and good pay, and where everybody treats you as if he expected you wanted to be honest, and make a man of yourself; and no police stealing on your tracks to take you to the watch-house, or rich folks pulling their clothes closer about them as you pass, for fear they would be soiled by the friendless news-boys.

" 'Mrs. L—— and all my friends here think the Lodging-House is a great institution ; and they say I ought to bless God that I ever found the way there.

" 'I believe I have told you all the news, and as my hand is tired I must now close my letter.   Yours, very affectionately,

SAMMY J——.' "

The voice of the Superintendent had scarcely ceased before the boys cried out:

"Hurrah for our old friend Sammy!"

"Long life to him!" shouted little Paddy, in his excitement turning a somerset over a stool. "Long life to him! and to all as is kind to the news-boys!"

"Here is a letter," continued Mr. Rogers, "from a gentleman with whom Ernest Cowles was placed. You remember dear little Ernest?"

"Oh yes! we remember him, with his long hair."

"And his sunny blue eyes," added the gentleman. "His was a sad case, so early left an orphan; but he has a happy home now. The gentleman says:

"'DEAR SIR: — My wife has for some time been urging me to drop you a line concerning the little waif you left with us. He is well, and is the happiest child I ever saw. We have

never been blessed with children, but I feel
for this desolate little boy the warm affection
of a father; and I do not mean he shall ever
want a father's care as long as God spares my
life. My wife feels just as I do; indeed, I can
say for her, that she never looked so satisfied
and happy as since she has had a pet upon
which to lavish her affections. We live in a
retired spot, on the banks of a beautiful sheet
of water. Ernest runs about the farm from
morning till night, — his hands and apron full
of flowers, fresh leaves, or weeds. Everything
is a wonder and delight to him. When I
leave home the thought of his childish joy
warms my heart; and when I return, I am
sure to see his smiling, happy face watching
at the gate for me, and hear his merry voice
shouting, " Mamma, I'm glad my papa has
come home."

" ' So you see, my dear sir, you can set your
heart at rest about your late charge, for he

has entwined himself closely about our hearts. God giving us wisdom and strength, we will train him up to be an ornament to society, and a jewel in his Saviour's crown.

"'We should be glad to know all that can be ascertained concerning his parents ; for though we wish now to make him forget that he is not our own child, the knowledge may be a comfort to him at some future time.

"'With many wishes for your prosperity in the glorious work which you have undertaken,

"'I remain your obliged friend,

C. JENKS.'"

Some other letters were read, but none excited the interest which these two did. The boys could do nothing for some time but talk about them, and wonder whether they should meet with such kind friends when the time came for them to leave the Lodging-House.

Mr. Rogers improved the opportunity to urge upon them the importance of diligent attention to their studies, to their business, in whatever they were engaged ; reminding them of the remarks of their friend the farmer from the West. The boy who is most industrious and persevering here, is the boy we want to build up our western country. Later in the evening Jack sought the Superintendent, and related to him the proposal made by the attorney.

Mr. Rogers was quite as much pleased as Jack had expected at the prospects which opened before him. During the evening he gave the lad much good advice concerning his conduct in his new situation.

"Remember," he said, "you have now an opportunity to make a character for yourself. If you sincerely and humbly implore God's blessing on your endeavors to please Mr. Sennott ; if you strive to be faithful to his interests, both on account of your gratitude to him, and because your Father in heaven requires it, there is no doubt you will succeed. You will have temptations from without, and temptations from your own heart. Be honest with yourself, so that every night when you lay your head on the pillow you can say, 'I have tried to do my duty.' "

CHAPTER XII

"WHERE do you go to church, Jack?" inquired Mr. Sennott a few days later, as he sat warming himself before the blazing fire.

"To Dr. S——'s," was the rather proud reply. I have attended the Sabbath School there for many years."

"And does Edward Norris go too?"

"Yes sir, and the Hollands."

At this very moment the door was thrown open, and the pennypost tossed in two or three letters.

Jack sprang from his stool to pick them up, when he saw one was addressed to "*Mr.*

156

John Stetson, office of E. O. Sennott, Esq."
He blushed as he glanced at it, for this was
his first letter, and therefore exceedingly
welcome.

He tore the neat envelope rather awkwardly,
and found it contained an invitation to a wedding in Dr. S——'s church. Accompanying
the invitation was a beautifully printed card,
on which were the names of Frederick Sears
and Edith Holland.

Jack carefully replaced the whole in the
envelope, and passed it to Mr. Sennott.

"What!" exclaimed the gentleman, "Sears
and Holland? Why, I had no idea your
friends were connected with that old firm."

The young clerk repeated what little he
knew of their history.

"The same — the very same," responded the
lawyer. "I remember well when this young
man left his home because he disapproved of
his father's course; and would not, as his

father wished, connect himself with the business."

On his way to dinner Jack ran into the street where Mrs. Holland lived, but found she and her daughters had removed the day following the return of Mr. Sears. He was obliged, therefore, to content himself with anticipations of seeing them at the wedding, which was on the following day.

He found Edward also had received a card, and was greatly excited by it.

Though fully sympathizing in the joy of their friends at their returning prosperity, yet it was natural that these youth should feel rather sad when they reflected that there could be no more social evenings, no more unity of sentiment, as when both parties were struggling amid poverty and want.

The next morning, when, attired in their best suits, they entered the church, just as the bridal procession were alighting from the carriages, they realized more than ever how wide was the difference between them, — two poor unknown youth just entering on the stage of active life, and this handsomely dressed party after whom all the crowd were so eagerly gazing.

Never had Edith look so lovely. A brilliant spot burned in the centre of each pale cheek; her lashes veiled the lustrous eyes; and their was an expression of calm happiness on the pure white brow, and around the small well-cut lips which arrested the attention of the beholder.

The bridegroom was a man of noble proportions and a face stamped with benevolence; while his manner toward the lady by his side proved that the marriage on his part, at least, was one of the truest affection.

Louise, attired like her sister in white satin, leaning on the arm of a young gentleman, a stranger to both the boys, followed the bridal

pair, while Mrs. Holland was supported to the
pew by an elderly gentleman, with white, flow-
ing hair.

When the ceremony was concluded, the
young men saw Louise glance quickly around
until her eyes fell upon them, when she spoke
in a low voice to her sister, who also looked
around, smiled, and bowed. They paused in
the entry to see the wedded pair pass to the
carriages, when, greatly to their surprise, both
Mrs. Holland and Louise came to them.

"You must follow immediately to Union
Square," cried the young girl. "Edith is going to Washington directly, and she made me
promise to invite you to dinner."

Before they had time to reply, she had taken
her place in the carriage.

They were ushered into a handsome parlor,
with heavy old-fashioned furniture arranged
round the walls, where the bride came quickly
forward to receive them.

"You gave us a dinner-party once," she said, smiling and looking very happy, "and now we shall hope to see you often at our dinner-table."

Notwithstanding all that was done to make them feel at home, Edward, and even Jack sighed when they thought of the quiet attic chamber, and were relieved when the hurry attending the departure of Mr. and Mrs. Sears gave them an excuse for leaving.

"I wonder," said Edward, as they were walking together toward their respective places of business, "how Louise, or even Edith can so soon become accustomed to their change of prospects. It is scarcely a week since they were living in one attic chamber; and now" —

"They are heiresses in their own right," interrupted Jack. "While that young man was talking with you, Louise told me all about it.

"I will give in brief the history she related.

11

Her father and Mr. Sears were half brothers
—children of the same mother, but not of
the same father. They were in partnership
together when Mr. Holland died. That was
their Uncle Sears's house, where Edith used to
spend more than half her time with her aunt,
who was sick. When Mr. Holland died, Mr.
Sears made out that the firm had failed, and
there was but a few hundred dollars left for the
widow of his partner. As he had possession
of all the papers, it was difficult to prove anything against him. Frederick his son, who was
greatly attached to his cousin Edith, suspected
something was not right, and urged·his father
to give his aunt the portion destined for
himself. Mr. Sears became very angry, and
threatened to disown his son if he ever said
another word on the subject. At last Frederick felt so indignant that he left home
suddenly, sending a letter to Edith that when
he had earned a home for her, he would come

back and take her to it. He had written repeatedly, but had never been able to gain any
intelligence from them.

"But when Mr. Sears was attacked with his
last illness, it seems he sent for his lawyer, and
directed him to make inquiries about Mrs.
Holland. Not being able to learn anything
about her, he wrote her a long letter enclosing
notes, deeds, and mortgages amounting to a
handsome fortune. He wrote also to his son
confessing the fraud he had practised, and im-
ploring him to search for his relatives, and
restore them their part of the property. The
reader is already acquainted with the means
by which Mr. Frederick Sears ascertained their
situation. The very next day he persuaded
his aunt to remove to his father's house — he,
in the mean time, taking rooms at the Astor;
and finally, obtained Edith's consent to an
immediate marriage."

"Do you think they will want to see us

now ?" asked Edward, when his companion had finished.

"I think you ought not to ask such a question," urged Jack, warmly. "They are too kind and good to forget their old friends. Still, we must remember that now they will move in a different sphere. I, for one, don't intend to intrude upon them often."

"Nor I," was the rather sad response.

A week or two passed after these events, and Jack still continued to sleep at the Lodging-House. Every morning he experienced some inconvenience from the crowded state of the long closet, which ran along the whole length of the room, and he determined to go earlier to the office that he might have time to dispose of some of the rubbish.

His conduct during these few weeks had been such as to win the entire confidence of his master, who secretly congratulated himself on having so faithful a youth in his employ.

Mr. Caswell had now returned, and though his manner was cold and eccentric, Jack considered him a friend. The clerk was present when the youth asked liberty to carry away a parcel of rubbish which had accumulated in the closet, and in his dry way remarked:

"I have known a worse place used for a sleeping-room."

"What do you mean?" inquired Mr. Sennott.

"My remark was a general one," was the only reply.

Jack, however, caught the idea at once. "Yes, sir," he said; "if you are willing, I could sleep in there."

The lawyer walked to the door and looked in. "We will see," he said, smiling, "how much of a room you can make of it."

Two days later Jack triumphantly exhibited the place he had cleared. Old junk, half-worn brooms, a missing hod, and the lost dust-pan had been removed, together with two large boxes which had contained books, leaving a clear space of about four feet wide and eighteen long.

Mr. Sennott agreed that Jack should keep his bed there, occupying the office during the night.

The case which had called Mr. Caswell to a different part of the state was still in court, and would be tried at the approaching term. Jack had copied several of the papers, and knew that it involved a large and valuable estate. It seemed to him to be a similar case of fraud to the one whereby Mr. Sears had deprived his partner's children of their property, only that the offence was in this instance committed by a young man.

A gentleman by the name of Ransom was appointed guardian of the property of two orphan children. He died suddenly, and his son, a man of dissipated habits, disputed the claim, declaring all the money had been already spent for their benefit.

For a long time the lawyer tried in vain to obtain some clue to these missing documents ; but Jack ascertained that Mr. Caswell had been successful in obtaining some papers important to the case. These were placed carefully in the small pigeon-hole at the right of the clerk's desk.

CHAPTER XIII.

IT is now time to describe more particularly the situation of Edward Norris. Notwithstanding his want of proper restraint and instruction in his early boyhood, he had, as we have seen, kind impulses, and many generous, noble traits. After his sickness in the Lodging-House, there was a decided change in his whole character. As he gained the confidence of the Superintendent, and compared his present conduct with that of the other boys, a feeling of pride began to arise in his heart at his own superiority.

This was to be sure so slight at first that it

168

was not perceived even by his watchful friend Mr. Rogers. But before he left for his new business as printer, that gentleman had a long talk with him concerning his future welfare, and closed his kind advice by saying: "You know, Edward, I feel the greatest interest in you as one of my earliest pupils, and that I only say it for your best good when I tell you to beware of self-confidence. The city is full of temptations to young men. Go where you may, you will be beset with them. If you depend upon your own strength for power to resist, you will certainly fail; while if you ask grace of your Heavenly Friend, you will have it.

"I have watched your course, my dear boy, and have been fearful when I perceived that you already looked down upon your companions as beneath you. When that poor fellow was carried off by the police yesterday, I read in your countenance the feeling, 'I despise

you.   I thank God I am not a thief, or drunk-
ard, or even as this outcast.' "

"I did despise the wicked fellow," burst
out the boy in an impassioned tone; "but I
pitied him too ; and I thought," he added, his
countenance softening, " that I might have
been in his place if it had not been for your
goodness."

" Say rather.for the overruling Hand which
led you to the Lodging-House," responded the
good man, deeply moved.   "That is the right
feeling, Edward ; and while you continue to
be actuated by it, you will be shielded from
many evils. Only one word more. Watch
your own heart. Examine yourself. When
you can retire to rest satisfied with the actions
of the past day, all is well ; but when conscience begins loudly to remonstrate, you are
certainly in danger."

Edward thanked Mr. Rogers for his interest,
and obtained permission to visit the Lodging-

House whenever he had leisure ; and then left, though with the feeling that the Superintendent had rather magnified the temptations to which he would be exposed.

" I know too well the little comfort there is in being a snob or a snoozer," he said to himself, " to try that game again. I'm looking forward to being boss in our concern."

Several weeks passed, and still the young printer could look the Superintendent frankly in the face when he spent an evening in his old home ; and indeed there seemed to be a marked improvement in his character. He was ambitious to excel in his business, and so fully won the confidence of his employers that they congratulated themselves on securing his services.

A small library of standard books was connected with the office, from which he was at liberty to select for his own reading, and then the evenings at Mrs. Holland's were always opportunities for improvement.

Jack also was a restraint to his friend. He always had such firm confidence in Ned's principles, and was so sure he would try to do what would please Mr. Rogers, that the latter felt stronger when in his company.

Connected with the boarding-house where they both took their meals, was a youth by the name of Arnold. This young man was affable and winning in his manners, of a most pleasing exterior, and, for aught that was known to the contrary, of firm moral principles.

When Edward first entered the boarding-house, he looked up to Arnold as a superior being, and was greatly flattered when the latter began to pay him marked attention. Sometimes at table Arnold would address his conversation to the new comer; and then again he would accompany him on his way back to the office — passing his arm familiarly through

Edward's, or talking in a patronizing way of his interest in the young men of the city.

After a few weeks, our news-boy found that his companion did not hesitate occasionally to mingle oaths with his conversation ; but he did it in such an off-hand, matter-of-fact way, as if such language was common among gentleman, that Edward was rather pleased than otherwise.

Once, indeed, when Arnold was unusually profane, even vulgar in his talk, his companion ventured to remonstrate ; when the young man burst into a hearty laugh, and, clapping Edward on the shoulder, exclaimed, " Come, now, none of your Methodist cant with me. You're too good a fellow to talk in that style. I'll bet a new hat against your old cap that before the end of two months you'll roll off the oaths equal to the best of them."

Edward sighed as he thought of Mr. Rogers's instructions, while the words of Scripture,

" the Lord will not hold him guiltless that taketh his name in vain," flashed across his mind.

That night he found himself comparing Arnold with Jack, much to the favor of the latter. His new friend was easy, gay, and good tempered, but his society certainly was no benefit. Edward half resolved to plead an excuse for not fulfilling an engagement he had made for a stroll round the city the next evening.

Arnold, however, would not let him off. He had an object to accomplish with the youth, and he was too persevering to relinquish it.

Edward had often wondered how Arnold came in possession of so much money, as he was in no regular business. When questioned on the subject, the young man only laughed, saying he had property in the bank. But now he thought he had the news-boy sufficiently in his power to render it safe to enlighten him.

As they strolled arm in arm through the

crowded streets, they approached a large building brilliantly lighted.

"How pleasant it looks in there," cried Arnold. "Let's go in a moment."

Edward could remember the time when he had hung about the doors of this very place which he dared not enter. The first feeling on being invited, was pride that his situation allowed him to do so; but this was instantly succeeded by the thought of the warnings Mr. Rogers had uttered against gambling-saloons, and he hesitated.

His companion read his feelings at a glance, and determined to give him no time to demur.

"Come along," he urged, drawing him forward; "what harm will it do you to be a looker-on. It's good fun, I assure you."

They drew near the bar, where a showily-dressed lady passed each of them a glass of wine, with a smile and familiar nod to Arnold when she received from him the money.

Entering an immense hall, they found small faro-tables scattered in all directions, while a long table for billiards occupied the centre of the floor.

Arnold passed all these till he came to a small table at the extreme end of the hall, where four young men sat deeply absorbed in play. He stood by silently watching them for a time, until the game was finished, and then one of them invited him to take a hand.

At first he made a show of refusing, but his objections were quickly overruled, and he seated himself at the table, where Edward soon perceived he was quite at home. No invitation to play was extended to the stranger, but he found occupation enough in watching others. At the close of the evening they retired, Arnold the winner of thirty dollars. As they passed out they approached the bar again, and Arnold paid as before for two glasses of wine.

"I have found out how you get your money," said Edward, laughing.

"Yes," said the other, archly, "I told you I had property in the bank."

"But I didn't imagine it was a faro-bank. How easy it seems to win thirty dollars! I should have to work more than a month for that sum."

"Oh, to-night I did not attempt anything. I merely amused myself. It is as easy to make a hundred, when I give my mind to it."

For a week or two after this Edward was quite uneasy. He began to be discontented with his situation, complaining that he never should be rich as long as he plodded on in a printing-office. Day after day as he saw Arnold so handsomely dressed, with plenty of money at command, he almost determined to renounce business, and win money as his companion did.

All this time Edward avoided Jack, who was

12

often obliged to take his meals at a later hour, and did not once visit the Lodging-House. At night, after repeated visits to the gambling-saloon, followed by other visits lower down in the paths of sin, he could not sleep. Conscience, that faithful monitor, was continually sounding in his ear these words, "Enter not into the path of the wicked, and go not in the way of evil men. Avoid it, pass not by it, turn from it and pass away. For they eat the bread of wickedness, and drink the wine of violence."

One month passed away, and Edward grew pale and thin. He lost his appetite, and felt no interest in his business. He began to loathe the society of Arnold, but had not strength to break away from him. He went one evening with Jack to the Hollands', but was constantly in fear lest they should question him concerning his habits. He felt sure guilt was stamped on his countenance. He was in this state of mind, too, when he received an invitation to Edith's wedding, which was the reason he enjoyed the occasion no better. He dreaded being alone with his conscience, and he dreaded also the company of those whom he had once loved. Sometimes he resolved to go to Mr. Rogers, confess his crimes, and ask advice as to his future course, but pride prevented. He remembered the parting counsel of the good Superintendent, and shuddered as he thought how true the words had proved. He was indeed in danger of ruin, both of body and soul.

CHAPTER XIV.

EDWARD IN TROUBLE.

ONE evening as Edward was walking with Arnold, he met Jack going to the Lodging-House.

"Come with me, Ned," said his old friend, cordially. "Mr. Rogers wonders where you are of late that you have not visited him."

"I can't,—I'm engaged," Edward began, glancing at Arnold, when he suddenly stopped. The good spirit was whispering to him, "Go; it may be your salvation."

Suddenly snatching his arm from Arnold, he caught Jack's hand, saying, "Yes, I will;" and without giving his companion time to remonstrate, walked quickly away.

" What do you know of that fellow ? " inquired Jack, when they had gone a short distance. " I never exactly liked his looks."

Edward's face was crimson. There was a terrible struggle going on within him. " Oh ! if I could only be as I was before I knew him," was the language of his heart.

" Shake him off, and begin anew," said conscience.

" But what will he and my new companions think of me ? And besides, I begin to fear my own strength."

" God will help you, if you only repent," suggested the gracious Spirit.

His companion began to wonder at his silence, and drawing Ned's arm within his own said, tenderly, " You don't look as happy as you used to when we were at the Lodging-House."

" No, I'm miserable," burst out the other; " and it's all owing to that wicked fellow I've left. I've done with him now. I'm determined on that. If you'll help me, I'll quit my boarding-place to be rid of him."

" I shouldn't think that would be necessary; but if you will tell me about it, I'll advise you as well as I can."

" Come in here, then, where we can be by ourselves."

As he spoke Edward pulled his companion toward the door of a brilliantly-lighted building, well known to be the resort of young men of dissipated habits. It was professedly a reading-room; but wine was always furnished in abundance, and later in the evening cards were visible. Here Ned, in company with Arnold, had taken many a lesson in vice.

" Where are you going?" inquired Jack, in surprise.

Ned smiled bitterly, as he said, " There is a room at the farther end of the hall where we can be alone."

Jack took one step forward, and then stopped.

" No, I can't go in there. How can I pray
' Lead me not into temptation,' if I run into
the very face of danger ? "

" Where shall we go, then ? "

" To our good, tried friend Mr. Rogers. If
you have been doing wrong, as I begin to think
you have from your knowledge of such places
as this, there is no one will advise you so well
as he. Come, don't let's lose a minute."

" But, Jack, what will he, — how can I ? "

" Don't stop to ask questions when you know
what is right. Mr. Rogers is the man to help
you out of your difficulty. Be honest with
him. Give up that fellow, and your heart
will be lighter at once."

Mr. Rogers was not in when they entered;
but fortunately for Edward, whose courage
already began to fail, he soon came in.

Jack walked boldly forward and greeted
him, while Ned hung back, coloring violently,
scarcely daring to raise his eyes. Here, in the

presence of his teacher, here where he had so often resolved to be a man, a good, useful man, his conduct for the past months seemed more aggravated in guilt than ever before.

The Superintendent noticed at a glance that all was not right with his former pupil; but he held out his hand with the affection of a father.

"We are glad to see you once more among us," he said, smiling. "Come in and see Mrs. Rogers."

"I want to talk with you, sir," faltered the poor youth, at the instant resolving to make a frank confession of all his sins. "Have you time to see me now?"

Mr. Rogers cast an anxious glance around the school-room. "I must try," he remarked, "if the case is urgent. Come down with me to the lodging-room. We shall be by ourselves there."

Ned pulled Jack by the sleeve to induce him

to follow; but the young clerk whispered, "You'll find it easier to tell all if you're alone with him."

It is not necessary to repeat the conversation which took place between this good man and his erring pupil. It is sufficient to say that, once having commenced his tale of temptation and crime, he did not stop until he had laid bare his heart to the view of this compassionate friend. One bright thought in the midst of his sorrow alone comforted him. Arnold had repeatedly tempted him to rob his employers in order to find means to win back what he had lost at the card-table; but he had resisted, and remained faithful to their interests. He thought he still had their confidence, and could remain in their office.

Mr. Rogers looked so grave and thoughtful when Edward had finished, that the youth argued that he considered his case a very bad one; but presently he looked up, with an encouraging smile.

"I was thinking of this Arnold," he said, "and wondering what was his inducement to lead you into sin. I believe I know him, though by another name. If he is the man I think him, he is employed by the gambling-houses to decoy wealthy young men to their ruin. Easy in his manners, of a handsome person, and affable in his address, he is exactly calculated to deceive unwary youth; but why he should spend so much time and pains with you, a printer's clerk, I find it difficult to imagine."

"I suppose he expected I should get money somehow," faltered Edward, coloring violently as he called to mind the various arts used to induce him to take bills from his master's cash-drawer.

"Well, now that I know the whole case, I hope I can do something for you," said the good man kindly. "I shall want to think of it and sleep over it; but in the mean time I advise you to have nothing more to do with Arnold. You were not wanting in decision when you were here. Be a man, and say ' *No*,' boldly and decidedly, when he invites you to accompany him. Does Jack know all this?"

"No, sir, nothing. He urged me to come to you."

"Ah, Jack is a fine fellow! and what is much better, he is a Christian. Come to me to-morrow night, and I will talk more with you."

For nearly an hour the two youth remained at the Lodging-House, renewing their acquaintance with their old friends, and listening to some of their speeches, after which they took leave together.

On their way home Ned insisted on repeating to Jack what he had confessed to Mr. Rogers.

I scarcely need say that the relation caused much grief to the latter, who had no idea his friend had wandered so far from the paths of rectitude. He gave Edward such good advice as he was capable of, and on his return home took occasion to thank God that he had been withheld by restraining grace from the commission of similar crimes.

Ned reached home much earlier than had been his habit of late, and was considerably surprised on entering his room to find Arnold there.

For one instant the young man seemed confused, and Edward was sure he heard a low-muttered curse on account of his early arrival; but in a moment the other advanced with perfect self-possession, and said, " I have a raging head-ache, and thought you would pardon the liberty I have taken with your room. In fact I was just going to lie down on your bed, my room-mate having company; so if you'd been a few minutes later you would have found me sleeping here."

This was said with so much apparent frankness that Edward could make no objection to the statement; but merely saying, " My head aches, too, and I'm going to bed," began at once to undress.

Arnold started to leave the room, but then turned, and opening his coat, asked, " How do you like this vest, Norris ? "

It was a rich black satin garment, stamped with small sprigs of blue flowers. Edward held the lamp towards it, and then answered, " It is very handsome."

" If you think so, I wish you would accept it," added Arnold, laughing so heartily that he showed all his white teeth. " I bought it to-day for seven-fifty; but I can't endure the cut; it confines my arms."

He took it off, and threw it carelessly on the bed.

Edward was exceedingly fond of dressing well, and pride at once suggested that the vest would be particularly becoming to him; but just as Arnold was closing the door, he called him back to say:

"I'm much obliged to you, but I'd rather not have it."

" Nonsense!" cried the other, without reëntering the room. " What's the use of such squeamishness among friends. I shall never wear it again; and as I cannot return it, the favor will be mine if you will make use of it."

Edward made no more objection. In truth he was secretly pleased. He locked his door, tried on the vest, walked back and forth before the glass, admiring himself in it, and then retired to bed. His heart felt lighter than it had for many weeks; and with a determination to follow the advice of Mr. Rogers, whatever it might be, he fell quietly asleep.

CHAPTER XV.

A T breakfast Edward observed that Arnold, who was noted for his punctuality at his meals, was not present. The landlady took this occasion of his absence to extol her boarder for his general conduct, and particularly for the promptness with which he fulfilled all his pecuniary liabilities. She glanced at Edward as if sure he would respond to this praise of his friend. But with the knowledge he possessed of Arnold's character, he could say nothing in his favor, and therefore was silent, and soon leaving the table hastened to his business.

It was seldom that his employers, who edited

191

the paper, were at the office at so early an
hour, their business requiring them to be up
until late; but on entering he noticed that
both the gentlemen were present, and not at
their desks.   They were standing together,
talking earnestly.

Throwing off his coat he was proceeding to
hang it on the hook as usual, when the senior
editor said, sternly:

" Norris, have you ever allowed your key to
the office to go out of your possession ? "

" No, sir, never.   You told me to be careful
on that point when you gave it to me."

" Well, sir, then we must hold you responsible for several hundred dollars that are
missing, since no one else can gain admission
to the office."

Edward stood like one bewildered.   He
could not believe he had heard aright.   He
looked the gentleman full in the face, his color

rapidly alternating from pale to red, his confusion strongly resembling guilt..

" I am glad you do not try to deceive us by
denying it," remarked the other gentleman,
gravely. " We trusted you fully, Norris, and
are grieved that we have been disappointed in
you."

" What did you say I had done ? " inquired
Edward, beginning to recover himself.

The elder gentleman glanced searchingly in
his face, and then answered :

" For some time we have been aware that
money was taken from the cash-drawer — "

" But you didn't believe I would steal from
you," exclaimed Edward, indignantly. " I
have never seen the inside of the cash-drawer,
except when you paid my wages."

" You interrupted me, sir. I was going to
say that last night Mr. Peirce and myself left
bills here [touching the drawer] to the amount
of two hundred dollars, after having marked

13

them, so as to be readily identified. Now as
we were here until a very late hour, and you
alone were possessed of the means of entering,
we are reluctantly brought to the conclusion
that you are the thief."

"You have no right to conclude so exclaimed Edward indignantly. Some one might
have broken in — "

He stopped suddenly. A confused recollection of hearing some one in his room long
after midnight, and of the sound of a key
dropping to the floor, flashed through his mind.
Could it be Arnold who had stolen the money?

"I see you hesitate, Norris," was the sorrowful retort.

"I confess I hoped better of you; but, as it is,
I may as well tell you that a gentleman, one
too who takes great interest in you, called
yesterday to put us on our guard, — to beg us
not to place temptation in your way. It is
true, as he says, that we ought to have remem-

bered that your reformation bears recent date,
and that we ought not to have trusted you as
we have done."

At this point Edward sat down and covered
his face with his hands.

"This is the work of Arnold," he said to
himself. "He has done it to ruin me, that I
need not be believed if I should try to expose
him. Oh, how I wish Mr. Rogers were here!"

"Confess and return the money, and we
will allow you to return to Mr. Rogers," suggested Mr. Pierce kindly.

"I have never taken one cent of your money
— but I think I know who did," faltered the
youth, without removing his hands. "I was
just wishing Mr. Rogers were here."

"Pshaw!" said the other partner. "We
shall think none the better of you for trying
to throw the blame on another."

He called his partner aside, and after a few
words hastily left the office.

"You had better confess," urged the gentleman. "Mr. Wells has gone to procure an officer to examine your room. Unless you are worse than I think you are, he will find there the evidence of your guilt, and you will be arrested at once. I don't think you can have disposed of it so soon."

"I am glad they have gone ; I would have given them the key to my trunk," exclaimed the poor youth, looking more hopeful than he had yet done. "I am sure they cannot find it, because I have not taken it.

"Will you please, sir, tell me who it was that warned you against me."

"I don't know his name. He was a fine-looking man. He is a good friend to you, and did it for your good."

"I should think he did!" and the youth laughed bitterly as he felt more sure there was a plot laid to ruin his character.

"If you will send to Mr. Rogers, he will tell

you about it," he urged, as the other regarded him with wonder.

" We will wait the issue of the examination," remarked the gentleman, seriously.

He returned to his desk ; but as Norris occasionally glanced toward him, he saw that he was unable to fasten his mind to the duties of the day.

The more he reflected upon Arnold's conduct, the more Edward became convinced that he was the man who had brought this disgrace upon him, and a desire for revenge burned in his breast. He determined to take the first opportunity to enlighten his landlady as to the true character of her boarder, but immediately the thought arose, " Shall I, a convicted thief, be believed? Will my testimony be taken against him ? "

His thoughts grew more and more bitter. Though confident nothing would be found in his room which could be a witness against him ;

yet he was sure that if Arnold had resolved to
fix upon him the character of a thief, he would
find some means to do so.

In the mean time his employer, though apparently engaged in writing, was watching him
closely.   His readiness to have his room, even
his trunk examined, certainly did not look like
guilt.   Then he called to mind the remarkable
sobriety and faithfulness of the youth ever
since he had been in their employ.   He had
come to the conclusion that they had been
hasty in making a charge on the suggestion
of a stranger, that though well meaning his
principles were not firm, when, at the end of an
hour, Mr. Wells, accompanied by a police officer, came hastily up the stairs.

"I hope you have not let him escape," he
exclaimed, addressing his partner in an excited
tone.   "We have found abundant proofs of
his villany.   Locked in his trunk was a paper
containing all the marked money, with the ex-

ception of sixteen dollars, and in the closet my new vest, that I missed last week."

Edward, who had been hidden by a huge pile of paper, groaned aloud. He felt giddy, and thought he was going to die ; but the officer, who had seen him all the time, and who disliked scenes, put an end to this by dashing a tumbler of cold water in his face.

"What have you to say for yourself now ? " asked Mr. Wells, in a scornful tone, holding the vest up before him.

"I could tell you how I came by it, but you would not believe me," retorted Edward, springing to his feet. " I know how the money came there, too ; at least I feel sure myself, though I cannot prove it. Mr. Pierce, if you will send for Mr. Rogers, I think he can explain it all to you, and convince you that Arnold, the man who came here to warn you concerning me, is himself the thief."

Edward spoke eagerly, his cheek flushing,

and his eye frankly meeting that of the officer.

".Well, let's hear your story," said Mr.
Pierce, more than half convinced of his inno-
cence.

"I had rather Mr. Rogers would hear it,
too ; because he knows some facts which I only
suspect. If you, sir," speaking to the officer,
"will have the kindness to go with me, I will
ask him to come here at once."

The gentlemen spoke together a moment,
and then the officer signified his readiness to
accompany him.

They went down stairs together, but had no
sooner reached the door than Edward, without
stopping to request his companion to excuse
him, dashed back again to ask Mr. Pierce to
look from the window and tell him whether
the gentleman who was slowly passing was the
one who had pretended such friendship for
him.

The editor, after a glance, acknowledged that he was.

"I knew it," exclaimed Norris, greatly excited. Turning around he found the officer close at his elbow.

"You are such a slippery fellow," he said, "I must keep you in sight."

"I wouldn't part company from you at present," answered Edward, smiling; "for I want to see whether you are acquainted with a man who just crossed the street. Come, if we hurry we shall overtake him."

He put his arm through the officer's, and soon came in sight of Arnold, who, with his tiny cane, was switching the air as he slowly sauntered along the sidewalk.

"There he is — the one with the cane. Do you know him?" asked Edward, in a low tone.

"I rather guess I do," answered the man, with a sly wink out of the corner of his eye.

"Well, I'm pretty sure — as sure as I can

be without the proof — that he stole the money; for he gave me Mr. Wells's vest for a present only last night, and I found him in my room when I went home from the Lodging-House."

He then related facts with which the reader is well acquainted, and his suspicion that the noise he had heard in his chamber at midnight was Arnold putting the money in his trunk.

"More likely he went to return the key," remarked the officer, shrewdly. "I've had my eye out in his direction for some months, and 'twould be better than a good dinner to me to catch him tripping."

Finding that he had an interested listener, Edward went on narrating many incidents in his own life connected with Arnold; but neither of them could imagine why, with such pretended friendship, the villain had turned so suddenly against him, unless he had intended to keep the money.

"I wish I had asked Mr. Wells to see how

it was marked," cried Edward. " Perhaps he discovered the mark, and feared it would be traced to him."

" I rather think you've hit the nail on the head," responded the officer, laughing.

CHAPTER XVI.

EDWARD REINSTATED.

MR. ROGERS readily consented to Edward's request; and, after a few private words with the policeman, with whom he was well acquainted, came to the conclusion that this was a plot of Arnold's to get money ; but, finding it marked, deemed it more prudent to deposit it with Edward.

That the officer judged Edward to be innocent, might be inferred from the fact that he allowed him to remain out of sight while they were talking.

When they reached the office of the Commercial Advertiser, Norris gave the gentleman an account of his connection with Arnold, ending with the gift of the vest the night previous, and the noise he heard in his chamber.

They thought the proof against Arnold, combined with what Mr. Rogers knew of his character, sufficient to warrant an arrest, and the officer in company with Norris proceeded to his boarding-house for that purpose.

"If we could only get proof," repeated the man again and again. "This story sounds very pretty; but when they get the scoundrel into court, he'll be acquitted for want of proof."

Edward was silent from disappointment. He hated Arnold, and scarcely less strong was his desire for his own acquittal than for the conviction and sentence of the villain to a long term of imprisonment.

The girl who answered the bell was one to whom Edward had showed many favors. She had aged parents in Ireland, and as she could not write, he had several times exercised his talent for her benefit. Indeed, once he had printed a short letter for her, much to her delight.

Her face was very red, and her eyes swollen with crying; but as soon as she saw Ned she threw up her hands and uttered an exclamation of joy.

"And ye aren't in prison after all!" she exclaimed; "I was going to beg an hour of mistress, and let ye out. I could do it; and I would, if I lost my place by it."

"What do you mean, Ann?" he inquired, eagerly. "How could you let me out?"

She gave her head a toss as she answered, "I mean what I say; and money can't keep me from doing a good turn for those who have been good to me."

"Is Mr. Arnold in the house?" inquired the officer.

"No, sir, he is not; bad luck to him."

" Well, I will walk into the parlor. I want to ask you a few questions."

" Are you going to take him [pointing to Edward] to prison, sir ? "

" Either he or Mr. Arnold must go. One of them has stolen money from the office of the Commercial Advertiser."

" Och, indeed ! Mr. Norris sha'n't be put in the dirty place, for I'll go into court against the other. I saw him do it."

" Do what ? "

" Put the money in Edward's trunk ; " touching his arm.

· " Ah, that's evidence with a witness," re-marked the man, drily. " What is your dinner-hour ? "

" Two o'clock."

" With your leave I'll wait here then," tak-ing a seat where he could see who entered the hall without himself being seen.

"Is that what you've been crying for, Annie?" asked Edward, in a low voice.

"Well, it's no use denying it, 'cause it's the truth. I was dressing the bed, when I heard a step coming softly up the stairs, and then some one tried the door, to know whether it was locked, I suppose. I'll not deny I was frightened, and hid behind the bed; but I saw Mr. Arnold come in and go straight to your trunk, which he unlocked after trying a good many keys. Then he opened his own pocket-book and took out a great roll of bills, did them up in a bit of paper, and laid them in.

"That will do the business for Norris," he said.

"I was simple enough to think it was giving you the money, he was; but when the officer came to search your trunk, and I heard mistress say you was found out to be a big thief, I cried then. As to the vest, I can swear I saw Mr. Arnold wearing it at supper-time, so perhaps he put that there too. And if he didn't, sure, sir, turning to the officer, a vest is a small thing to put a bye in prison for."

"He shan't go into prison this time," responded the man. "I've done with both of you till the trial; so you had better go about your business."

"You shan't lose anything by crying on my account," whispered Edward, as they left the room. "I'll give you the prettiest book I can find at the stores."

I cannot stop to give a minute account of the trial and imprisonment of Arnold, alias Dale, alias Wingfield. Suffice it to say, he had been an object of suspicion in certain quarters for a long period, and did not receive much favor from the court. He was sentenced to hard labor in the state prison for the term of five years.

Edward Norris was honorably acquitted by his employers of all participation in the

14

theft. The cordiality with which they shook his hand on his return to the office proved their pleasure in being able to retain him in the office.

But the young man, though greatly relieved by the happy turn in his affairs, could not at once decide to return to business. He plead truly that his mind was so confused that he could not apply himself to labor, and they, though at great personal inconvenience, felt obliged to allow him a day or two for recreation.

The evening found him again at the Lodging-House. He had been disappointed in not finding Jack at home; and as he could not now as formerly pass an evening at Mrs. Holland's, he knew no other place where he could find that sympathy which was indispensable to his happiness.

Mr. Rogers received him with marked kindness. Mrs. Rogers congratulated him on his early release from trial, and the boys who had learned his story got up three hearty cheers for their old companion.

They invited him to make a speech, as this was club night; but he felt quite unequal to the effort.

At last, after some debating, a youth by the name of Standish was chosen orator for the occasion; and, mounting the platform, he commenced in the following strain:

" Boys, gentlemen, chummies: P'r'aps you'd like to hear sumwit about the West, — the great West you know, where so many of our old friends are settled down and grown' up to be great men — maybe the greatest men in the country. Boys, that's the place for growin' Congressmen and Governors and Presidents. Do you want to be news-boys always, and shoe-blacks, and timber merchants in a small way by selling matches? If ye do, ye'll stay

right here in the city; but if you don't, you'll
go out West and begin to be farmers; for the
beginning of a farmer, boys, is the making of
a Congressman and a President. Do you
want to be rowdies and loafers and shoulder-
hitters? If ye do, why ye can keep around
in these diggins. Do you want to be gintle-
men and independent citizens? You do?
Then make tracts for the West.

"If you want to be snoozers and rummies,
policy players, and Peter Funks men, why
you'll hang up your caps, and stay round the
groceries, and jine fire-ingines and target com-
panies, and go firing at hay-stacks for bad
quarters; but if ye want to be the man who
will make his mark in the country, ye will
get up steam and go ahead, and there's lots on
the prairies a waitin' for ye's.

"You havn't any idea of what ye may be
yet, if ye will only take a bit of my advice.
How do you know but, if you are honest

and good and industrious, you may get so much up in the ranks that you wont call a gineral or a judge your boss? And you'll have servants of all kinds to tend you, to put you to bed when you're sleepy, and to spoon down your vittles when you are gettin' your grub.

"Oh, boy! wont that be great! Only think, to have a feller open your mouth, and put great slices of pumpkin pie and apple dumplings into it. You will be lifted on hossback when you go for to take a ride on the prairies; and if you choose to go in a wagon, or on a 'scursion, you will find that the hard times don't touch you there; and the best of it will be that if 'tis good to-day, 'twill be better to-morrow.

"But how will it be if you don't go, boys? Why, I'm afeard when you grow too big to live in the Lodging-House any longer, you'll be like lost sheep in the wilderness, as we heard of last Sunday night here, and you'll maybe not find your way out any more.

" But you'll be found somewhere else. The best of you will be something short of judges and governors, and the feller as·has the worst luck, and the worse behavior in the groceries, will be very sure to go from them to the prisons.

" I will now come from the stump. I am booked for the West in the next company from the Lodging-House. I hear they have big school-houses and colleges there, and that they have a place for me in the winter time. I want to be somebody, and somebody don't live here, no how. You'll find him on a farm in the West, and I hope you'll come to see him soon, and stop with him when you go, and let every one of you be somebody, and be loved and respected. I thank you, boys, for your patient attention. I can't say more at present. I hope I haven't said too much."

A long-continued shout of applause followed this speech, after which another youthful Demosthenes arose; but one of the audience sat as if spell-bound. There were perfect roars of laughter, and cries of "Hi, now! that's the talk, old fellow!" but Edward heard them not. To him the words of the first speaker came with peculiar power. He had often listened to similar appeals, but never when they came home to his own heart. He had considered his destiny decided, and himself settled in the city for life; but now, discontented with his present situation, unwilling to be longer in the employ of those who had even suspected him of defrauding them, unwilling also to subject himself to the temptations of a city life, which had proved too much for him, his thoughts turned to the great and growing country whose claims upon his attention his friend had so forcibly portrayed.

His ambition was fired at the thought.

" Who knows but I might rise to be a Governor, or even a President? Or, if not, I might amass great wealth, and become a useful, honored citizen. I will try it, — yes, I will go."

Before he left the Lodging-House Edward sought Mr. Rogers, and informed the gentleman of his new-formed resolution, and was not discouraged when the reply was, " I will think of it and sleep over it."

As for himself, though he retired early, he scarcely slept at all. His wonder was that he had not thought of this plan before. He resolved to make an early call upon Jack, and inform him of his new project, and then to notify his employers that he wished to leave their services.

" It is their own fault," he said, his face burning at the recollection of the charge that had been made against him. " They preferred to trust a stranger rather than one who had served them faithfully for months."

Here his conscience smote him. "I committed sins against my Maker quite as heinous," he said, half aloud; "and what restrained me from being really what I was charged with being, a thief?" Nothing but the grace of God, which Mr. Rogers talks so much about.

"Well, there wont be half the temptations at the West. I am determined to go."

Messrs. Pierce and Wells were very reluctant to have Edward leave them, having experienced much difficulty in getting trusty youth in their office; but when they found his determination was fixed, they interested themselves in his future prospects, wrote a letter of high recommendation, and gave him a handsome suit of clothes, including the vest already spoken of.

He remained in the office, however, for three weeks, and then went to the Lodging-House, where he devoted himself to his studies for nearly a month longer; at the end of which time a company of young men went West, under the care of Mr. M——, who succeeded in finding good places for them.

CHAPTER XVII.

EDWARD'S NEW HOME.

PERHAPS I cannot give the reader a better account of Edward's situation and prospects than by quoting from a letter which he wrote Mrs. Rogers about two months after his settlement in his new home.

"R——, Ill.

"My Dear Friend : — I suppose you will wonder that I have not written you ; but after Mr. M—— called to see me I was very busy, and then I thought I would wait till I could tell you something encouraging about myself.

"I suppose Mr. M—— told you that the gentleman who took me is the owner of a large

219

farm, and that he raises hundreds of acres
of wheat and corn and oats. I reached here
just in time to be of good service to him, and
though at first it was all new to me, he says I
learned to plough, harrow, and sow seed faster
than any boy he ever had.

"Mr. Monson has several children, and he
treats me as if I were one of them. The
daughters too, are very kind to me, and one of
them, seventeen years old, takes care of my
clothes and keeps them in nice order. Though
she, her mother, and all the family work hard
a part of the time, yet they are educated people. They moved to Illinois from Connecticut.
Mrs. Monson and her daughters play the piano,
and Sabbath nights we have a grand sing.
They insisted that I could learn if I wished.
Now I have got so I can join in some tunes.
Every morning and evening we all go into the
sitting-room for family prayers. No matter
how busy we are, Mr. Monson says no one ever

lost anything by giving God his due ; and certainly a half hour morning and night is not much to devote to thanking him for all his mercies. We all read a verse in the Bible, and then sing a hymn while one of the daughters plays (most generally Lucy), and then Mr. Monson offers a prayer.

" Somehow I can't help thanking God at such times for what he has done for me.

" When I think what I was once, and what I should have been but for the kind people who got up the News-boy's Lodging-House, I feel that if ever any one ought to thank God, it is I. But when I remember how wickedly I forgot all he had done for me, and all your kindness, and how I committed so many sins, I sometimes think I'm too far gone to be forgiven.

." One day I felt very badly. Mr. Monson and I were working alone about two miles from home. He saw I looked sober, and he asked me if I was sorry I came West.

"'No, sir-ee,' I said. 'I've enjoyed more since I came than all the rest of my life together.'

"'What is it, then?' he asked; 'I've thought you seemed rather down-spirited for a day or two.'

"It came right into my mind then to tell him how I felt. He dropped his hoe and sat down under a tree, and there, right on the ploughed land, he prayed God to pardon all my sins, for the sake of Jesus Christ. He told me I needn't feel at all discouraged. All I'd got to do was to tell the Saviour what a sinner I'd been, and how sorry I was, and that I wanted him to forgive me.

"Dear Mr. Rogers, I hope some time I shall be as good a Christian as he is. If I am, I shall try to do everything I can for poor orphan boys.

"I try to be faithful in my work. Mr. Monson says he is more than satisfied with me.

We have horses in abundance, and I can ride about wherever I please. The farmers here never ride without a span, — and fine horses they are, too.

"Mr. Monson has promised I shall go to the fair this fall. It is a great occasion out here. It will be my own fault if I am not a rich man and a useful man.

"Before I close my long letter, I want to thank you and all those benevolent individuals who formed a society for taking friendless, homeless, and often wicked children from the street, and training them up to be good and useful citizens. Certainly if any men deserve a blessing they do. If many of those wealthy merchants who live in luxury and roll at their ease in their splendid carriages would consider the wants of the poor and how much crime might be prevented by educating the children to good habits, I think they would be far happier to give a portion of their money to the good work. Certainly when they come to die they would be happier than if they had spent it all on themselves.

" Mr. Monson wishes me to say, ' God bless you ever in your noble work.'

" Your affectionate, obliged scholar,

EDWARD NORRIS."

Here we must leave Edward for the present, and return to our friend Jack, whom we left fast winning the confidence of Mr. Sennott, and the attorney engaged in preparing a case in court — Morrill versus Ransom.

Passing over a period of several weeks, we find Jack has not only made himself of great service to his employer, and proved himself honest, industrious, shrewd, and discerning, but he has also advanced quite rapidly in his studies. His manner of spending the day was this.

He rose early, and after removing his mattress to the closet, for time was precious with

him, lit the gas and sat down on the rug before
the fire to study his Latin for fifteen minutes,
so that he might have something to think of
while making the fire and putting the room in
order. Sometimes it was to decline a noun or
conjugate a verb ; sometimes to commit a list
of irregular verbs, such as sum, volo, fero,
edo, fio, eo, and their compounds, with an occasional glance at the book ; so that by the
time his work was done, quite a good lesson
was learned. When the clerk came in, he ran
away for his breakfast ; after which he copied
papers, went errands, or did any other business required of him. At half-past one he
went to his dinner, where he had a pleasant
chat with Ned, then back again to write or to
study, unless Mr. Sennott motioned to him that
it would be more improving for him to listen
to some explanation of law. Then tea at six ;
when, except for an occasional visit with Edward to the Lodging-House, or attendance at
15

the weekly lecture, where he was sure to meet the Hollands, he had a long and uninterrupted season for study.

When Mrs. Sennott sent his mattress and bed clothes, he had begged for some large pieces of cloth to cover the table and sofa; and these he was in the habit of spreading over the furniture at night, as also to have his hod for the cinders and his kindlings ready for morning.

As the lawyer insisted that the closet was too small to sleep in, he always brought his bed out and spread it next the wall behind the sofa, which at this season was pulled up toward the fire.

One night, having studied rather longer than usual, he fell into a profound slumber, which was at last disturbed by the click of the lock on the door. Repressing the inclination to scream, he put both hands to his heart to stop its wild beating, and soon heard steps cautiously entering the room. By the shadow from their lantern, he perceived there were two men come, as he supposed, in search of money. As cautiously as possible he slid from his mattress and crept under the sofa, where, lifting a corner of the large covering, he could see all that passed. It was fortunate for him that the light used by the robbers was what is called a dark-lantern, throwing the rays on objects directly before them and leaving the rest of the room in shadow.

Jack was ignorant whether there was much or any money in the desk. At one moment he thought he would with a sudden start throw open the window and call loudly for the police ; then he resolved to wait and watch. The latter resolution was quickened by hearing one of the men say, in a hoarse voice :

" The papers will be marked, of course."

" Yes," responded the other ; " and if we can but destroy them, we're safe enough."

"It's a risky business, though," suggested the first speaker, rummaging among the papers. "I hope you'll make good your promise to me."

"Here they are!" screamed the other, with an oath, and without waiting to answer the question. He turned toward the light to read more distinctly, and thus Jack for the first time plainly saw his face. "Here they are!—'Morrill versus Ransom'—all arranged and marked for the trial." He laughed a low, malignant laugh, in which the other joined. Ha, ha, ha! wont they look blank to-morrow? Come — luck has favored us — let's be going."

"We may as well relieve the lawyer of any loose change," said the other man, taking a small instrument from his pocket and easily picking the lock to the desk.

"Pshaw!" exclaimed the other, with an angry oath. "What a fool you are. Don't you see that when they find the lock has been forced

they'll have the police on the scent at once.
Now we've thrown away the four or five hours
that were in our favor; for they'll search at
once to find what's missing."

Here the man grew so enraged that Jack
feared they would get to fighting before they
left the office. His lips were perfectly color-
less, and he clenched his hand, holding it in the
face of his companion. But with a seeming
effort controlling himself, he muttered some
indistinct sentence, and then repeated the
words, " Come — it's time we were off."

The door was scarcely closed when Jack
bounded out of bed, thrust his feet in his
pants, and seizing his outside coat hastened to
follow the robbers down the stairs, carrying
his boots in his hand. They were hurrying
along the street, and he cautiously followed,
taking care to keep in the shade of the build-
ings.

When they had gone the distance of two or

three streets they stopped a moment, said a few words, which he was not near enough to hear, and then separated. From their conversation, however, he had learned that the taller man was the principal in the theft, and the other only the hired accomplice. He did not hesitate a moment, therefore, in following the first, which he did, up one street and down another, until, in his half-dressed state, he was chilled through. But suddenly the man stopped at the door of a mean-looking house, and, taking a night key from his pocket, passed in out of sight.

Jack, who knew the locality well, only stopped long enough to make sure of the number and the general appearance of the place, which he was able to do by a neighboring street-lamp, and then ran with all speed back to the office. Here, falling on his knees in front of the fire, he fervently thanked God for protecting his life from danger, and rendering him the means of bringing the iniquity of the robbers to light. By a rapid association of ideas, too, he went back to the time when he himself had been guilty of theft, the one instance of which, it will be remembered, he had confessed to Mr. Sennott. He shuddered when he thought that unless withheld by the overruling providence of the kind Being who had watched over him, he might now be spending the hours of darkness in perpetrating deeds of villany. Never before had he felt so convinced of his need of Divine help to keep him in the path of right, and never had he so earnestly implored the God of his mother to be his God and portion forever more. He sat there in the dim firelight, tears streaming down his cheeks. He remembered how his mother used to be comforted and soothed by giving her cares up to her Saviour, and he for the first time experienced this kind of peace in his own soul. He knew not how it was, but he felt that God was now his Father and his Friend in a manner he had never been before. All his cares for the future faded and vanished away in the calm trust that filled his soul. He knew that whether poverty and want, or prosperity and fame, such as had heretofore been the dearest wish of his heart, were his portion, all his steps would be ordered for him in infinite mercy.

A neighboring clock striking three, re-called him to present duty. He realized that it was important Mr. Sennott should know of the loss of the papers as soon as possible; and yet he feared if he should rouse the gentleman at this hour he might be charged with unne-cessary haste. But the trial was to take place during the day which had now commenced, and the missing documents were all-important. He shuddered as he thought they might al-ready be destroyed; and though he would be obliged to leave the room free to any one who might wish to enter, as the lock was gone, he resolved to delay no longer.

The family of Mr. Sennott were not a little startled at being aroused from sleep by the loud and continued ringing of the door-bell.

" Who's there ? " called out a servant from the upper story, and " Who's there ? " called the lawyer from below.

" I want to see you, sir," Jack remarked to the last questioner.

" Can't you wait till morning ? "

" No, sir ; I must see you *now*."

" Well done, my young fellow ! " exclaimed the gentleman, as, after having listened to Jack's rapid account of the robbery, he cordially extended his hand. " From your description I conclude the midnight thief to be Ransom himself. And so they thought to stop proceedings, hey ? " This was more to himself. He laughed in derision, but then said,

"You must be hungry, Jack. I think I can find something to satisfy you."

"Oh, no, sir! And I must be back at the office, which any one can enter — only I thought you ought to know, sir."

"Well, run, then, and get an hour of sleep. By six I shall make Ransom an unexpected visit in company with an officer, and shall wish you to go with me and identify the thief."

Jack was soon on the rug again, but he felt no disposition for slumber.

"What a night this has been to me!" he said repeatedly, — "a night I never shall forget. If mother can see me, she will be happier, even in heaven, to know I have begun to love Jesus."

He hastened to renew the fire, and have all ready before Mr. Sennott came. Then, as it was still dark, he lit the gas and read a few verses in the Bible. Heretofore he had scarcely opened this volume, except to read occasionally a story on the Sabbath, or to commit his Sabbath-school lesson. Now it seemed the dearest treasure he had on earth — his chart to heaven.

After again committing himself to the care of God, he went into the closet, and took from the chest where he kept his clothes a little pocket-book which his mother had used. Here he kept his small amount of money. This he carefully counted, and was greatly pleased to find that it contained sufficient to make full restitution to the lad from whom he had stolen some papers nearly three years before.

Just as the clock struck six, Mr. Sennott, the clerk, and an officer entered.

CHAPTER XVIII.

JACK AND HIS SAVIOUR.

THE police officer examined critically the door lock, then the fastenings to the desk; after which he made Jack repeat the description of the two robbers. To tell the truth, the lad had not paid much attention to the accomplice. He had not thought it worth while, when the principal was by. The officer shook his head. It was evident he thought otherwise.

" There was nothing, then," he said, at length, " by which you could recognize the other ? "

" Nothing, sir, except his singular voice."

236

" Ah," said the man, with a smile. " He had a peculiar voice, then ? "

" Yes, sir : it was sometimes low and hoarse, then it would rise high and seem to be beyond his control. I noticed it even in the few words they said at parting."

" And he was short and stout ? "

" Yes, sir. But I did not say so."

" And had a stoop in his gait, like this ? "

" I remember that, too."

" He wore a brown surtout, and striped pants ? "

" Oh, no ! His coat was blue, with loose sleeves, which seemed much too long for him. I don't remember about his pants ; but his sleeve caught in the cover of the desk when the other was so angry with him : that was why I noticed it. They were lined with red."

" Ah ! "

The officer was growing pleased with himself, and made the exclamation in a tone of great self-complacence.

" Why do you care so much for him ? " Jack asked, simply.

The man regarded him a moment in silence, and then, with a glance at the others, said, " It is likely he took the papers."

" No, sir ; I think — I am almost sure — he did not. The tall man found them and held them firmly in his hand. If he has not kept them he has destroyed them, and not given them to the other."

" I think so, too," said Mr. Sennott, speaking for the first time.

They went out together, and proceeded directly to the street where Jack had been the night before. The officer explained his plan of taking the criminal as they went along. Here again Jack was to be made useful. Instead of ringing the bell, which might startle the inmates at this early hour, the lad was sent round to the back door, to tell the servant that a man at the front wanted admittance. Once inside, the officer would ascertain Mr. Ransom's room, while Mr. Sennott and his young clerk stood at the foot of the stairs to prevent the criminal's escape.

Everything happened as they wished. It was but a third-rate boarding-house, and the servant stupidly answered the door without asking Jack any questions. Without a word she directed the officer to the first door on the second flight, and then opened into a basement below, motioning the others that they might go in there if they chose.

But they had not long to wait. It seemed scarce a moment after the policeman entered the chamber before they heard a loud shriek, followed by a noise as if a table had been thrown over. They rushed to the rescue.

"Is that the man?" asked the officer, pointing to a ghastly-looking object seated on the floor a soiled handkerchief tied around his head for a night-cap, having made an extremely hasty toilet.

Jack gazed, but did not speak. He could not bear the thought of testifying against a man merely on suspicion, and he certainly did not recognize him.

"Pretty strong circumstantial evidence," the officer went on, clapping his hand on his breast pocket. "Papers all safe here! Now, young man, you just run down and send me here the first police officer you can find; and you may save yourself as a witness for his trial. He'll be better dressed, maybe, then."

The trial went on. The counsel for the defendant wondered at his absence. Presently Mr. Sennott summoned some witnesses, when Mr. Ransom and his midnight accomplice were led in by two men with stars on their breasts. Mr. Sennott alone seemed unmoved. The opposite counsel started to his feet and demanded an explanation. The lawyer briefly stated, " Your client has been arrested on a charge of breaking open by force my office, and wrongfully seizing papers to which he had no claim. These papers are essential to my case."

Then the judge called for a reading of them. Mr. Ransom's head sank lower and lower on his breast. The other criminal looked around with a defiant air.

By and by Jack was called to give his testimony, as the judgment of the other case rested on the authenticity of the papers, and the motive the criminal had for seizing them. On hearing this, the men both started. Mr. Ransom was asked whether he had anything to say. He made no sign. The man with the hoarse voice was then interrogated, and tried in.vain to command his tones. Jack recognized them both, and came first-best out of the trial, having received an approving nod from his master, and a commendation from the judge for his

16

prompt course of action. He went home feeling very happy.

Contrary to his custom Mr. Sennott returned to the office from the court, instead of going directly to his house. The clerk was out, and the gentleman, after seating himself before the bright fire, sat for some time smiling to himself. Jack was finishing a paper the clerk had given him to copy. When he had done, he saw the gentleman deliberately take out his pocket-book and count one, two, three bills.

" Here, Jack," he said, smiling again. " Here is the money for your clothes. You can have no scruple about taking it now, for you have well earned it."

" I did not think of being paid, sir," was the blushing reply.

" Nevertheless this is your due"—thrusting the money into his hand.

When he had gone, Jack found himself possessor of thirty dollars.

The excitement and fatigue of the previous night prevented his sitting up late to study. When he lay down on his humble couch to rest, he did so with the sweet assurance that Jesus his Saviour was with him : his preserver, his guide, his elder brother. Through all the scenes, the cares, and excitements of the day, this one reflection which brought him peace ; " Jesus is mine — I have chosen him ; he bought me and I am his," followed him every-where.

" I must tell Edward," he said to himself. " I must try to bring Edward to love my Saviour."

Then he reflected how pleased Mrs. Holland would be that his mother's prayers had been answered, and he brought to repentance and faith in Christ. He loved her more than ever. He loved all the people of God. There seemed to be a new tie formed between him and Mr. Sennott. Oh, how happy he was !

He awoke the next morning wondering whether Mr. Caswell was a Christian. Before he had made the fire the clerk knocked at the closed door. He noticed something unusual in the glance with which the youth regarded him, and presently said :

" You made a good day of it yesterday."

" Yes, sir."

" I mean you made some powerful friends. Mr. Sennott told me what the judge said."

Jack looked full in his face a moment, and then with a slight blush said, " Yesterday, or the night before, I gained the best friend I ever had."

" Indeed, and who was that ? "

" Jesus, my Saviour. He has promised to be my friend forever."

The clerk gazed a moment at the lad, then shrugged his shoulders and turned away. But he did not readily forget.

CHAPTER XIX.

JACK AN ACTIVE CHRISTIAN.

FROM this time the old friendly feeling between Alfred and the young clerk revived. The youth came often to his father's office, and never seemed better pleased than when Jack was at leisure to talk with him.

Mr. Sennott watched the growing intimacy, at first with some anxiety. Alfred, the last one of five children, had been carried through the sicknesses to which children are heir only by the most tender nursing ; and even now the disease which had so early carried off one and another seemed ever ready to appear. Alfred, therefore, was the darling of his pa-

245

rents; and it was no wonder the lawyer should carefully guard him from the least injurious influences.

But Jack could not live day after day as he now tried to live by the rules of the blessed volume which had carried his mother to the gates of paradise, without winning the entire confidence of his employer. It soon became evident to him that Mr. Sennott was pleased with the influence he was obtaining over the young lad, and resolved that by the grace of God this influence should be used only for good.

Thus more than a year passed — Jack, or John, as Mr. Sennott invariably called him, growing constantly in the affection and esteem of the whole family. He now had a room next to Alfred's in the lawyer's house, and took most of his meals there. This was first brought about during a short sickness of Alfred, when he was constantly mourning for his companion. Within a few months, too, he had begun to attend the Latin school. But with all this attention and advancement the lad maintained his former humble manners, and was even more respectful and attentive to the wishes of his benefactor. He continued to take care of the office, and to render all the aid there by way of copying which his studies would allow. To Edward he was the same earnest, devoted friend, even more devoted than formerly; for, until young Norris went to the West, he did not fail to urge him to give his heart to the Saviour.

During the third year of Jack's connection with the lawyer, the symptoms of consumption, which had so alarmed Alfred's parents and the family physician, became more confirmed. The mother's heart sank within her as she heard the hollow cough, and saw the bright hectic flush which every afternoon beautified the checks of her darling boy. These were too familiar signs. She knew, alas! too well what they betokened.

The insidious disease which the physician said had for a long time been undermining the constitution of the sick youth, now progressed alarmingly. The incessant expectoration, the dry, hacking cough, the fearful night sweats, the swollen limbs, followed one another in quick succession until it was evident to all that Alfred was fast approaching the world of spirits.

It was all in vain that the parents hoped against hope, — that they tried to persuade themselves this attack was only a severe cold like others through which he had lived and recovered to his usual health. The fiat had gone forth. Alfred, the last loved and perhaps the best beloved, must die.

So overwhelming was this affliction that neither Mr. or Mrs. Sennott at first perceived that Jack had left school, and was seldom absent from the bedside of his young friend.

They had become so accustomed to seeing him there and considering him one of the family that they did not realize his worth to his sick companion until one morning when the clerk sent him out of town on an errand which occupied him the entire day.

"Where is John?"—"I want John to read to me"—"I wish John would come home," were words uttered many times before he returned. It was all in vain his mother offered to read, to talk, to do anything for his comfort. No one but John could do what he wished; and the mother was at last inexpressibly affected to find that John was missed on account of his prayers and talk about Jesus the friend of sinners.

Time and again bending eagerly over the sick youth, while the nurse nodded in her chair, had Jack repeated the story of his finding his Saviour on the eventful night when the the office was robbed; time and again — for the stories seemed ever fresh and ever new — did Jack reiterate the account of the blind man restored to sight by his faith in Christ; the restoration of the prodigal to his father's love by penitence and confession of his sins; and the wonderful salvation of the thief on the cross, simply by believing that Jesus had the power to save him.

Mr. Sennott indeed offered many fervent prayers for and with his son; and the mother expressed repeatedly her hope that he would make his peace with God. But to Jack was given the precious privilege of pointing the weary soul to the haven of rest ; of knowing that he cordially embraced Jesus Christ as the Saviour of sinners — that he joyfully looked forward to a blessed eternity with him in heaven.

The end came at last, and all was peace. A few minutes before he breathed out his soul to God, Alfred, who was lying on his father's breast, feebly reached forth his hand, and, grasping that of Jack, placed it within his mother's, at the same time gasping with difficulty the words, " He will — be your — son. "

" Yes, yes, Alfred ; your wish shall be gratified," both father and mother responded.

A bright smile spread all over the pallid countenance ; then he whispered the words, " Pray for me."

Soon all was over ; but as the stricken parents gazed on that marble form, they thanked God that they still had a son.

And truly in after years they were grateful that the desolate void made in their hearts was filled by the loving, dutiful attentions of their adopted child.

The year after Alfred's death John went to college, where the early discipline he had received was of great use to him. He was studious, and faithful, and gained the cordial affection of his classmates.

Our young friend was now much improved in his personal appearance, — his earnest, soul-lit eyes, and his hair, which still waved over his forehead as of old, being all that would remind one of the little news-boy.

He was simple and unobtrusive in his manners, even when he had abundant wealth lavished upon him, and when he had attained a high standing in his class; but he owned to himself that his besetting sin was pride. Though his reveries were somewhat more reasonable than when at the Lodging-House he used to imagine Mr. Sennott introducing him as " Hon. John Stetson, your Senator," yet they often led him a wild chase far into the future. At such times he would unlock a small trunk which he constantly kept at the head of his bed, and take from it the suit of clothes he had worn when he first met his kind benefactor. These, made for him by his mother from a coarse suit of his deceased father's, were worn threadbare, and patched with a variety of colors. But how well he remembered the effort it had cost the sick woman to render them fit for service, when there were no means to procure others.

The sight of these garments never failed to soften his heart, and call forth gratitude to that kind Being who had watched over him from his infancy, and guided his steps to such a pleasant path. On leaving college his adopted father gave him a few months to decide upon a profession, at the same time intimating the pleasure it would give his parents should he choose the law.

John was for some time undecided between this and the ministry, but finally acceded to the wish of his kind friends, and entered Mr. Sennott's office once more as a candidate for the bar, to which in due time he was admitted, with great honor to himself, amidst the prophccics of his friends that he would attain to eminence in his chosen profession.

About the time Mr. John Stetson was admitted to the bar, Mr. Rogers received the following letter from Mr. Norris, from whom, through all these years, he had kept up an occasional correspondence.

"MY DEAR SIR: — Having an hour or two of leisure this evening, I think I cannot spend it more pleasantly or profitably than by writing you.

"I am sitting in my own parlor surrounded by a farm of one hundred and forty acres, well stocked with horses, cattle, sheep, and poultry. More than all this, I have as good a wife as there is in the United States, and a chubby boy of six months that I would not exchange for all the wealth of your city.

"I often wonder as I review the ways of God with me. Left a poor, homeless lad, glad to make a meal from the refuse of the streets, or to find a lodging beneath a cart, what would have become of me had not the overruling hand of a kind Heavenly Father watched over me and directed me to the news-boys' happy home.

"I was particularly led to this train of reflection by an incident that occurred at our last county court, when I happened to be a juryman.

"A man was arrested for stealing horses and an attempt to murder a gentleman who disputed his claim to one of them.

"I thought when he was brought into court that his countenance looked somewhat familiar, and taxed my memory to recall where I had seen him. His name, he said, was George Brown ; but he proved to be my old acquaintance Arnold. I don't think he recognized me until I was leaving the Court-house. A servant from the hotel was holding my spirited horses at the door, when some one addressed me as Mr. Norris. He turned from the officer who was leading him to prison, and gave me a searching look. Poor man! how I pitied him!

"The next day I visited him in his cell. For a long time he was sullen, and refused to answer my questions; but at length his curiosity was aroused, and he asked me, with an oath, how it was I had become so rich.

"When I told him that it was by my own persevering industry, with the blessing God promised every honest laborer, he laughed in my face. He insisted that I had married a fortune. I told him my wife's father built and furnished our house; but beyond that every cent was my own earnings, — though I had made a good deal by the rise of land near my farm.

"He seemed very thoughtful after this, and before I left confessed if he were fifteen years younger he would try his luck on a western farm.

"I did what I could to urge upon him the claims of God, but could not see that I made much impression. I have been twice since, but he has refused to see me; so now I must leave him with One who has power to turn the hardest heart.

"As for myself, though I am painfully conscious of falling far short of my duty both toward my Maker and my fellow-men; yet I do try in my humble way to show that my religion is not all in my profession.

"My wife, who is a very devout woman, is a vast help to me in my Christian course. I have often told you how religiously she was brought up, and we strive to order our little household according to the pattern of my good father-in-law Mr. Monson.

"I thank you for the reports. They come to us like old friends. My wife is as interested in them as I am. I only hope every poor

17

child in your great city will find a friend as
kind and faithful as you have been to me.

"Don't you ever think of taking a vacation ?
If you do, remember that I, as one of your
earliest scholars, have a great claim on you.
Believe me, dear sir, you would he welcomed
with the affection grateful children feel toward a kind parent.

"Please give my regards to my old friend
Stetson. I am rejoiced to hear of his success.

"Yours, very gratefully,

EDWARD NORRIS."

About a month later Mr. Norris wrote again :

"MY DEAR SIR : — I have had reason to know
of late that life is made up of checkered scenes
of joy and sorrow. My wife's mother died last
week, after a short but severe illness, leaving
her husband only the hope of spending an eternity with her in praising God to sustain him in
his deep affliction.

"There is one daughter at home old enough

to keep her father's house, but she will be obliged to have some one to assist her about the work. There could not be a better place for the poor orphans; and after talking it over with my wife I have concluded to visit your city and bring back a young girl, if a suitable one can be found. My object in writing is to request you to give my letter to the Matron of the Girls' Lodging-House, that she may select a child if possible before I reach the city.

" Excuse me for troubling you with this; but I am sure you will be glad to assist in rescuing one more poor child from the haunts of vice, and placing her where she may be taught her accountability to God, and how to support herself in an honorable manner.

" Yours, truly,

EDWARD NORRIS."

And now before I close my story I must say a word concerning the widow Holland and her daughters, as their acquaintance had so important an influence on the character of our news-boys.

Louise Holland married and removed to the West, while her mother, now an elderly lady, whose snow-white cap and gold-bowed glasses were the delight of her little grand-children, continued to live with her daughter Mrs. Sears.

Of the latter it is sufficient to say, that, having learned by painful experience the suf-ferings to which the virtuous poor are exposed in so large a city, she spent much time and money for their relief.

In after life, when listening to the throng of news-boys singing their monotonous song under her window, she often repeated to her children incidents in the life of Jack and Ned, so intimately connected with her own, and thanked God for the blessed institution which had done so much for this growing class in our community.

www.ingramcontent.com/pod-product-compliance
Lightning Source LLC
Chambersburg PA
CBHW031926060726
47496CB00007BA/2104